THE DARK SIDE OF THE MOUNTAIN

CHRISTOPHER MARS

ILLUMIFY MEDIA GLOBAL
Littleton, Colorado

Published by
Illumify Media Global
www.IllumifyMedia.com
"We bring your book to life!"

Library of Congress Control Number: 2020920914

Paperback ISBN: 978-1-947360-70-9
eBook ISBN: 978-1-947360-71-6

Typeset by Art Innovations (http://artinnovations.in/)
Cover design by Debbie Lewis

Printed in the United States of America

CONTENTS

FOREWORD

Christopher Mars and I met in 2016. We soon discovered a shared passion: Colorado. Chris has skied since the age of six, climbed forty-eight of Colorado's fifty-four 14,000-foot summits, and completed the Pikes Peak Marathon and Triple Bypass cycling tour. As a Colorado native, I also am enthusiastic about Colorado's history and its high country. I am a retired defense and intelligence worker who is an amateur military historian and board member of the 10th Mountain Historical Display Group. Chris also is into World War Two history and, particularly, the 10th Mountain Division, whose roots lay in Colorado.

As historians, we face a constant dilemma: how to get the layperson to be as passionate about history as we are. Perhaps the reason many people claim they do not like history is simply because the format with which it has been presented to them. Textbooks tend to be boring or dry. But history is anything but boring and dry. The popularity of films such as *Titanic* or *Gladiator*, the historical inaccuracies of these movies notwithstanding, are proof of that.

The story of the 10th Mountain Division in World War Two is an extraordinary one. And Chris tells it well. The 10th was the only US Army division to recruit skiers, back woodsmen, mule skinners, and the like. Working high in the Colorado Rockies, they trained in skiing, rock climbing, and winter survival. Because they were a one-of-a-kind unit, the Army waited until the right place and time to send them into combat. And that place was in the Apennine Mountains of northern Italy. The Germans held the high ground and had trapped the US 5th Army in the valley below for months. Scaling a mountain the Wehrmacht deemed unclimbable, the 10th Mountain Division seized the high ground at night, held it—desperately at times—and freed the 5th Army to push the Germans north, until their surrender on May 2, 1945.

In *The Dark Side of the Mountain* Chris has personalized the exploits of the 10th Mountain Division. After years of thorough research from the division's historical timeline to the training and equipment used Chris has opened a window into the "forgotten front" of Italy, which has largely been ignored or rendered unimportant. . This entertaining story of the 10th is a story of redemption and hope and the power of faith and friendship,. It brings history alive to the average reader. You will not be disappointed.

Michael Voelkelt
Board Member of the 10th Mountain Historical Display Group

1 - THE BEST LAID PLANS

"With traffic and weather together on the tens, this is KOA NewsRadio, and I'm Scott Kelly. Back to our earlier story, still no word on those missing snowboarders, last seen Thursday evening on the University of Colorado campus in Boulder. The Clear Creek Sheriff's Department and Rocky Mountain Rescue continue to search the area around Berthoud Pass, and stressed their determination to find the missing men before the approaching storm."

Shit! thought Pete McGregor, wiping his sweaty palms on his ski pants, at war with himself. Again.

In a month and a half you'll be seventy-eight years old, Pete, he told himself. *Haven't you done enough penance? You've helped rescue a lot of people in the high country, for a long time, decades. At your age, you're more of a liability, and you'll probably get someone killed. Put your ghosts to bed.*

To hell with you! the other half of his conscience responded, in protest. *I may not be as strong as I used to be, but I'm still an expert skier.*

Yes, but seventy-eight is still old.

I'm as fit as most men half my age.

You're brittle, old man.

Pete pounded his fist on the dashboard. He passed a bare hand through the silvery crew cut perched on his head, then rubbed his hand across his chest. Some of the chiseled muscle still remained, but most of it sagged now. He felt the shameful jiggle of his old flesh, even beneath his parka. He thought he was at peace with the loss of his strength, but there were times, like now…

Nuts!

"What am I doing up here, God?"

He waited to hear the Almighty's voice.

No response.

"If You have any words of wisdom, I'm ready to listen."

Silence.

Pete talked to God a lot. When God spoke back, the voice always sounded like Pete's. But after all these years, Pete knew how to tell the difference between his thoughts and God's. God always seemed to speak at the right moment, be it a comfort or a damn pain in the ass.

Earlier this morning it was the latter.

Pete had awoken during a dream at 3:26 a.m. (or did he wake *because* of the dream?). Two young snowboarders, missing for several days. College kids. *Probably out-of-staters, with no flippin' clue about the danger of the high country!* thought Pete when he first heard about it.

There, lying awake in bed, his mind at full throttle, he knew trying to go back to sleep was futile. So he slipped out of the bed he shared with his wife of forty-nine years and five months and plodded softly down to the kitchen of his Breckenridge, Colorado, home, to make coffee and consider what to do next. He drained the first cup and was pouring the second when God spoke.

"Go rescue those snowboarders."

Pete spilled some of the coffee he was pouring. Sweat formed on his upper lip as he cleaned up the mess.

I'm too old now, God. Look at me. In my younger days? No problem. Now?

"My grace is sufficient for you. I know the thorns in your flesh."

Pete was afraid God would say this. He knew better than to argue. It was a matter of faith. And faith in God mattered more to Pete than anything else.

He dressed in the dark of his bedroom, careful not to wake his wife, who always needed a lot of sleep, even at this age. Then he packed his gear quickly—his emergency checklist, laminated and always stored in the same spot, as well as his emergency pack, ever filled and ready to go, made this relatively easy.

The sky was still completely void of the coming day as Pete sped north on Highway 9, toward I-70, careful of the wet road and the icy bridges. The growl of his truck's V8 and his own thoughts were his only companions.

Now here he was, up on Berthoud Pass, ready to trudge "over hill, over dale," as Shakespeare would say, to try to do what even the professionals had been unable to do: find two college-age needles in the haystack of the Rocky Mountains.

He was thinking of the note he'd left for his wife on the kitchen counter, ashamed of its brevity, when one of the behemoth orange snowplows of the Colorado Department of Transportation disrupted his thoughts, splattering the side of his idling truck with the snow it scraped off the highway.

Snow peppered the window of his old Ford Bronco, there in the parking lot of the defunct Berthoud Pass Ski Resort. Unable to relax his white-knuckled grip on the worn steering wheel as he waited for the sun to come up, he glanced the long-odorless pine tree air freshener hanging from the rearview mirror.

I meant to replace that thing weeks ago. What is wrong with me? Why am I so forgetful? Dang it, I hate getting old!

He pulled a flask from the pocket on the inside of his parka. Inlaid on its silvery side was the emblem of the Tenth Mountain Division, with the words *Italy 1945* etched beneath it. Pete swirled the liquid inside.

"God, grant me the serenity to accept the things I cannot change, the courage to change the things I can, and the wisdom to know the difference," he prayed aloud.

He placed the flask in his truck's glove compartment and rolled down his window. An icy blast of wind smacked his warm face. He rolled up the window, turned off his engine, and retrieved his flask, stuffing it back inside his coat. He got out, marshalled his gear from the back of the truck, and put it on as quickly as prudence would allow, afraid he'd change his mind if he didn't hurry.

As he attached the climbing skins to his skis, he thought about where he should search. He hoisted his pack to his shoulders with the kind of grunt only an old man knows. Shivering, he searched for his goggles, but he couldn't find them.

Crap, I knew I was forgetting something!

He put on his sunglasses instead, despite the darkness, hoping they'd offer some degree of protection from the ceaseless wind. Pete thought briefly about heading east from the parking lot, but something in his gut told him the snowboarders went the other direction, across the two-lane highway to the runs and bowls on the west side of the pass. Towing his orange plastic sled behind him, he headed in that direction, toward the Continental Divide.

Slowly he plowed through a foot of fresh powder. There were no other tracks. Half an hour later, at the top of one of the gentler, abandoned ski runs, he took a water break. The western sky was gray now, and in the east, behind the Indian Peaks, the sky flared orange.

By late morning the sky everywhere was clear and deep blue. The wind had died down, but the cold air still stung his nose and lungs. He wanted a sip from his flask.

"God, grant me the serenity to accept the things I cannot change..."

He scanned the two big bowls of snow above him.

Which one? The two snowboarders most likely only had time to ski one, maybe two, even if they hitched a ride back up the pass. And if they disappeared, then either they both probably hit a tree or rock and were killed or they triggered an avalanche. So either both are dead, both are injured, or a combination of each. This will be rescue or recovery. Either way, I need to find out.

A short time later it was time for lunch. As cottony bursts of clouds drifted by, Pete found a low-lying rock with some small, knotty, bristly pines clinging to it, and hunkered down in the lee as best he could, preparing to eat, trying not to think about his longsuffering wife, back in Breckenridge, worrying about him. His hips and shoulders throbbed with pain, and his lower back ached. He swished a few drops of rum from his flask, then devoured some cheese and chocolate, his favorite backcountry foods.

His thoughts drifted back to his days long ago in the Tenth Mountain Division, training in Colorado, during the Second World War. He'd posted watch on countless snowy ridges, with his best friend, David Bates.

David Bates. When was the last time I thought of him? Only now, Dave, in my old age, do I understand you. You played your part in life well, old friend. Hell, how would I have made it through the war without you?

Pete drank some water, then splashed his gums with rum, savoring the sweetness. He rose slowly and scanned the sky. The sun was inching its way down to the western ridgeline, burning more and more daylight like the sticks in a pack of matches. Pete wondered if he should head back. But he pushed on, just a little farther. Surely he'd find signs of an avalanche soon.

Keep going, you can do it! came the voice in his head.

Pete stopped and cocked his head. *Did I just hear that or imagine it?* The air was still.

He pulled his binoculars from his pack, scanning ahead for signs of large slabs of snow that had broken away. Nothing.

Pete kept going, but not before another sip from his flask. The sun dipped behind the high wall of rocky, powdered peaks to the west. Ten minutes passed and Pete stopped again for another look. He focused on the most distant bowl he could see. And there it was: a long, narrow, partial slab of snow that had broken away from its northern edge.

Pete's heart raced. He pulled off his gloves and wiped each palm on his coat. The avalanche didn't appear to be a big one, but it funneled into a narrow-looking couloir, choking itself with snow while the rest of it disappeared into the trees, about five hundred feet below. He searched the chute for signs of life: movement, clothing, equipment. Nothing.

But he had to know for certain. It appeared that he could drop down the ridge, to the north and west, and circumvent a clump of trees, but he'd have to stay high. The thought of having to head down the narrow chute knotted his stomach.

Pete dropped off the high, windswept ridge, following the route he'd planned. He didn't quite stay high enough on his descent, dropping a bit too far down. He ended up having to sidestep up a snow field for about a hundred yards to avoid the patch of evergreens guarding the chute. He trudged to a spot above the trees and fell to the ground, his head spinning from exhaustion. Five minutes later it seemed to take all his energy just to get back up.

The bowl was right in front of him now. Sure enough, the far side of it looked as though it had just been scraped clean. The chute below looked bigger than Pete initially thought, but it was still clogged with snow from the avalanche. The snow was most likely stable now, so he decided to take the risk of skiing on it.

But what about the snow back up in the bowl that hadn't broken loose? It could come tumbling down at any time. He wasn't sure his body could hold up, but the sky was beginning to lose its light and every minute that went by meant the lost snowboarders were closer to death, if they weren't dead already.

Pete leaned on his ski poles and waited silently. He bowed his head and shut his eyes. A gust of wind kicked up and light, dry snow swirled briefly around him, dancing on his cheeks and lips.

Keep going!

The voice in his head spoke so clearly that he glanced over his shoulder, certain someone was standing behind him. But he was alone. In the recesses of his mind he knew it was God's voice, but he tried to convince himself otherwise.

"What? God, is that You again? It'd be nice to know for certain. I'm afraid here."

Images of the Garden at Gethsemane filled his head. He pulled off his pack, dropped to his knees, and prayed as quickly and earnestly as he knew how.

Sweating, his mouth dry, he fished his flask from his coat.

"You won't need that, Peter. It will diminish you. You have what you need."

"Either that's You, God, or the voice of my AA sponsor. Which is it?"

Silence.

Pete let out a deep sigh and slowly stuffed the flask deep into his pack. Then he stripped the climbing skins off his skis, carefully folded them up, and stowed them away. When he slung his pack, it seemed like it weighed half a ton. Then, as the dusk gathered around him, he clipped his sled harness back on, gulped, said another quick prayer, and dropped into the lower half of the high bowl, heading for the chute below.

He made his turns as quickly as he could, but his old, tired legs couldn't make them fast enough. The sled was heavy, and he hit the chute with too much speed.

"Help me, Lord!" he forced from his throat, in a voice resembling heavy-grit sandpaper.

His skis rocketed out in front of him, taking on a life of their own. Suddenly Pete was merely along for the ride.

He panicked, straightened his downhill leg too much, and tumbled over. He rolled and slid down the couloir faster than he thought was possible, and knew he was in trouble. Desperate pleas to God forced their way from his throat. His skis popped off, and he lost his poles as well. The sled broke loose and rolled over and over. He couldn't break free of his pack, though, its weight adding to his rapid plummet and the straps limiting the use of his arms. The trees in the glen below, the ones the avalanche failed to reach, were coming up fast. He had to try to slow himself down before he impaled himself on a branch.

Somehow he thought of his ice axe, which was strapped to the side of his pack, and reached for it. He grabbed it, then lost his grip.

He reached again. No luck. He had one more chance before he smashed into the trees!

He grabbed for it, found the blade, held tight, and yanked it free of its strap with all his might. He held it to his chest, one hand on the top and the other on the shaft. Then he rolled over, onto the axe, and dug the blade into the snow as hard as he could. The axe plowed into the fresh snow. It didn't seem to work at first; then all of a sudden his speed fell off, and before he knew it, he came to an abrupt halt, about a dozen feet from the nearest tree.

He rolled over once more and gulped in the frosty air, sweat rolling down his forehead. His shoulder and his lower back felt as though they were on fire, and he was afraid to move. Then he gingerly slipped his arms out of the straps of his pack. His shoulder felt marginally better, but every time he moved, pangs sprang from his back.

Okay, that did not go well, Pete. And now you're a wreck, ya idiot! What the hell are you doing here, anyway?

Pete sat up, and the pain in his back intensified. He opened his pack and fished around inside. He found the flask, twisted the cap off as quickly as his cold, arthritic hands would allow, and took a few gulps.

"Nuts! What the hell am I doing here? I'm out of control. Everything's out of control. It's all a big mess now, God! FUBAR!"

Just then Pete thought he heard a distant voice. He forgot about everything and sat motionless, straining his ears. It was dead calm. Then he heard it again, from down below, somewhere in the trees.

"Hello?! Is anyone there?!" Pete shouted, rising to his feet.

"H–help me! Please help me!"

"It's okay! I'm coming! Hang on! Don't move!"

Pete gazed about, looking for his strewn equipment. His skis, poles, hat, and water bottles looked like a yard sale gone wrong, and he scrambled about to collect them. His sunglasses were nowhere to be seen. His sled lay a short distance away. His legs began to post-hole into the deep snow as he pursued his belongings, but the going was much tougher than he'd hoped. He kept shouting into the woods below.

"Hang on! I'll be there in just a minute! Just give me a minute!"

Finally, he got his equipment together, put on his skis and pack, attached his sled, and headed into the gathering darkness of the forest.

"Where are you?! Give me a shout so I can find you!"

"I…I'm here in the trees! I'm further down from you, I think!"

Pete struggled to control his speed in the dense glen, and he had to stop frequently. Tree branches scraped his clothes and his pack, crackling and snapping off.

He caught a splash of color in the trees below. A moment later he glided to a rest beside a pale, shaking, crumpled hulk wearing a red parka, black snow pants, and snowboarding boots.

"Where are you hurt?"

"It's…it's my legs. I can't move them. They really hurt."

The young man told Pete his name was Travis and that he'd been lying there for a couple of days. Pete had to work fast to assess the severity of cinjury, treat it as best he could, and get him to some kind of shelter, before the incoming storm arrived.

"Were you with a companion, Travis?"

"Yeah. His name is Zach. We went looking for fresh powder, but I guess we triggered an avalanche or something. I tumbled over and over and must've blacked out. When I woke up, I was in a lot of pain and lying here in the woods. I called out for Zach a ton of times, but I didn't hear anything back. I hope he's okay."

Pete pulled off his gear and knelt beside Travis, applying gentle pressure to each portion of his legs. Suddenly, as Pete put pressure on the lower part of his legs, Travis screamed as though he'd been stabbed.

"I'm sure they're broken, Travis. And that means I'll need to make splints for you. So I need you to hang on a little longer. I can't move you until I stabilize your legs. I've got a couple of gadgets, called Sam Splints, in my pack. They're moldable, so they'll conform to your legs. Then I'll wrap them with some ace bandages I have."

Pete set Travis's legs, then gave him the strongest painkillers he had —an expired prescription he kept on hand "just in case."

He needed to build a snow cave, an impossible task in a glen. So he slapped his skins back on his skis and headed out, in search of an open space with at least some type of hill— anything with elevation that would enable him to dig in a horizontal rather than vertical direction.

"I'll be back soon, Travis. There's food and water and extra clothing in my pack, if you need it. Just let me know."

"Okay, thanks. I'm afraid, Pete."

"Sometimes I still get scared too."

Then Pete skied off, slowly weaving his way through the sharp, knotty trunks, in search of an open patch. He angled his path away from the fall line, hoping the glen wasn't too wide and that he'd stumble upon an open space or hillside. But after twenty minutes, with fading light and little progress, he turned around and struggled back up to Travis, breathing hard and beginning to stink of sweat.

They'd have to bivouac right there, in the open. Pete had an emergency space blanket, a couple of sleeping bags, a waterproof tarp, and extra clothing. He'd have to dig down into the snow and make a type of trench for them. It wouldn't be as ideal as a snow cave, but it would offer decent protection from the elements.

In the meantime, Pete gave Travis extra clothing: two fleece jackets and a wool watchman's cap. But as he was pulling the clothes out of his pack, his flask slipped out, plopping solidly into the soft snow. Pete thought he'd secured the cap on the flask. It was obvious he hadn't as the cap popped off and the caramel-colored liquid quickly spilled out, staining the snow amber. The flask gleamed dully in the fading light.

Wonderful! I'm sure I look like a damn drunkard.

"That was just a bit of rum, something to take the edge off every now and then. Just in case."

Travis's gaze remained fixed on the rum-stained snow as Pete spoke. Then he turned to Pete with eyes that radiated a familiar desperation.

Think fast, Pete!

"That was probably for the best, Travis. Alcohol and prescription meds don't mix well together. And besides, you could end up addicted and...addictions have a way of robbing people of their dignity and strength."

"If you say so, Pete. It's just that, well, my legs are really jacked up. I'm in a lot of freakin' pain."

"I know about pain, kid. But this is all a moot point anyway. That was the only alcohol I had. We'll just have to suffer without it."

Hope seemed to drain from Travis's eyes as his face turned ashen.

Pete couldn't find the right words to respond, and felt small. He placed a gloved hand on Travis's shoulder, smiled gently, the way he did with his grandchildren, and hoped it would suffice. Then he got his compact snow shovel and went to work constructing a trench as deeply as time, space, and light would allow. His pack thermometer read eleven degrees, but he was sweating after only a few minutes.

Pete glanced over his shoulder. Travis was rifling through his pack.

"Whoa, kid! What are you doing?"

"Nothing!" he said, quickly looking up. "I…I just wanted some food. You have some, right?"

"Yeah, sure. Next time just ask, okay?"

Pete gave him some beef jerky and a hunk of cheese, and went back to work. He jabbed his shovel into the snow and heaved it. Then he paused and turned back toward Travis, catching his eye.

"I just wanted food, Pete. Honestly."

"I don't know if I believe you. Just be truthful with me, okay? I'm trying to help you."

"Yeah, you bet."

Pete turned away and went back to work, slower this time, lost in thought.

"He's scared, Pete. And he knows nothing of faith. Be there for him."

Lord, that kid is going to get himself, me, or the both of us killed!

Silence.

Pete kept digging.

"You said the same thing to Dave Bates once."

Pete froze. A shiver ricocheted throughout his body even as a bead of sweat trickled down from his temple to his cheek. For a moment he stopped breathing, watching his last breath gently billow in the dense, cold air like a spectral cloud.

Then the memories washed over him. It was at Camp Hale, during training for the war. He and Dave were rock climbing. But he had trouble remembering more than these few details, shame smothering his thoughts like a cold, spring fog rolling off one of the Great Lakes.

Pete hurled his shovel into the snow like a spear.

Have I learned nothing, Lord? It's over fifty years later, and I still seem to be the same broken man I was back then. I just…I thought I'd left all that behind.

"Left what behind?"

My humanity, I guess. Pete sighed. *Sometimes I just don't seem to have what it takes.*

"I guess you'll have to rely on grace."

Pete nodded, resigned. His shoulders drooping, he picked up his shovel and finished the trench. He retrieved his ground cloth and spread one end uphill across the top of the trench to create a roof, and the other end, facing downhill, he suspended about five feet in the air, creating a type of ramp, so that in the event of a snow slide, it might act like a wedge to break up and divert the snow away from the trench. Then he secured the tarp by anchoring the corners to nearby trees, with small bundles of emergency cord he carried in his pack.

"How do you feel, Travis?"

"Pretty damn good right now," he said with a lazy smile.

"That's good, because I need to drag you into the shelter, and it'll probably hurt. You ready?"

"As ready as I'll ever be, right?"

Travis was built like a linebacker—burly but not enormous. His mop of jet-black hair contrasted with his fair skin, the way his stubbly beard did as well. His gray-green eyes seemed too narrow for his broad face and square jaw.

Pete grabbed the younger, bigger man beneath his arms, and pulled, to no avail. Pete couldn't move him.

Wow! How much does this kid weigh? 225? 230?

Then he tugged harder and slowly dragged Travis to the shelter. Pete felt a twinge in the middle part of his back, and he knew he'd pulled a muscle—another reminder of his age. But it was virtually dark now, and he ignored the pain in his haste.

He slid Travis into the far end of the cramped trench, where the shallow walls of dug-out snow were deepest and the most protected from the elements. He lit a candle, its dancing flame refusing to be snuffed out by the bitter, gusty wind.

Next, he needed to pick a flat spot to set up the backpacking stove. Though Pete flattened the floor of the shelter as best he could, it was still rather lumpy. So he picked a random spot and tamped it down even further. He lifted the small, aluminum windscreen that came with the stove, set up the stove, primed it, and lit it, little jets of blue flame springing to life around the burner. He filled a small pot with the cold water from one of his water bottles, placed it on the burner, and waited. It would take fifteen or twenty minutes, maybe more, for the water to boil at this altitude and temperature, so Pete entertained himself watching Travis devour many of the snacks Pete had brought with him: cheese, chocolate, fruit, pretzels, and his wife's oatmeal cookies. He was shivering a bit now, and Pete spread the space blanket across him.

"Those cookies are really good, Pete. Did you make 'em?"

"My wife did."

"Does she know where you are? Isn't she freakin' out about you?"

Ah crap! There it is again. Again. The one question I always get and the one I hate more than any other.

The ghosts of guilt and shame did their usual routine of haunting Pete, accusing him of being a bad husband, selfish and unloving.

"She's learned to accept it, mostly. We've been married a long time."

"I'm not trying to offend you or anything, but that sounds kind of selfish."

A heavy sigh escaped Pete's lips, matching the pain reflected in the wrinkles around his eyes.

"Yeah, Travis…I guess it is." Pete shook his head. "That's the thing about marriage. It's like an old bridge with a big truck rolling across it. Under a heavy load, its flaws get exposed."

Silence. Even the wind stopped for a moment. The only sound was the hiss of Pete's backpacking stove. It seemed to mock him, like an old-timey play where the crowd boos the villain.

"How about some dinner, Travis?"

"Sure, Pete. Those snacks you gave me helped a lot, but not totally."

"Let me check my pack; I can't remember everything I brought."

Pete scooted over to his pack and fished around inside, the bluish-white beam from his small headlamp dancing about.

"I've got a bunch of dried soup mix, in little Styrofoam packages. There's black bean, corn chowder, chicken noodle, beef chili, chili mac, mac and cheese, and, let's see,…one more, another corn chowder."

"Geez, Pete, what do you have in your pack? A supermarket?"

Pete let out a laugh. "Good one."

The water finished boiling, and both men enjoyed a hot cup of soup. Then Travis ate two more before Pete lectured him about conserving supplies. Not long afterward, both men prepared for sleep, Pete arranging heavy-duty sleeping bags for each of them.

"Where'd you learn to do all this, Pete? You look to be the same age as my gramps, and he could never do what you're doing. Shouldn't you be living in Florida and playing golf with other people your age?"

"I fought in the big one, Travis. They trained us to fight and survive in the mountains. The war ended a long time ago for me, but not on the inside. In war...you see and hear and do things that no amount of time will let you forget. Ever."

The only sound after this was the cold night wind whipping through the trees as both men slept.

2 - COCOONED

During the night Travis woke Pete up asking for some medicine for his legs and his pounding headache, as well as to urinate. Pete gave him more meds, then rolled him on his side so he could pee into the snowy wall of the trench. But this reminded him that he needed a bathroom break, too, and crawled out from the shelter toward a nearby tree, his headlamp guiding his steps.

Something moved in the trees, and Pete froze. The beam of his headlamp bounced off a pair of luminescent eyes that locked onto his, and he quickly found another spot to focus on, to avoid a direct gaze that the creature might interpret as a challenge. Pete spread his arms out wide and backed up slowly.

He was certain he left the snow shovel near the entrance to the shelter. *Shit!*

Pete kept one arm raised and an eye on the creature in the trees while he reached down, searching for the handle of his pack shovel, hoping it was sticking up from the snow nearby. He was near the shelter's entrance now, and found the T-handle of his shovel. Then the eyes moved in fast as the shadowy creature, a mountain lion, lunged at Pete from the trees.

Desperate courage rose up in Pete, almost thrusting him at the creature. He knew he'd have one chance to save his life and did his best to focus his strength and coordination. He cocked the shovel back, like a homerun hitter, and bashed the lion on the nose as hard as he could, then spun away and dove for the snow as fast as he could, trying to avoid the razor-sharp claws, but he was too late. His parka sleeve was shredded like tissue paper and warm liquid—he was instantly aware it was his blood—oozed down his arm. The big cat let out a high feline squeal, then hissed and darted into the woods.

Pete lay in the snow in a ball, his arms over his head. Seconds passed before he thought he might be okay. Carefully he lifted his head. There was no sign of the cat. Pete searched the dark woods fearfully. Nothing. He collapsed, facedown and gasping as though he'd just sprinted a hundred meters. The snow felt good.

"Pete! Pete! Are you okay? What was that?"

"Just...just give me a minute, Travis."

Pete got up, slow and dazed. He stumbled back to the shelter and searched for his medical kit.

"What was that, Pete?"

"Mountain lion."

"Oh my gosh! Are you okay?"

"I, uh, no. It got me on the arm. Got to find my first aid kit."

Pete did his best to focus on dressing his wound, but thoughts of infection, fever, and death played with his mind. Pete knew Travis wasn't the only one in trouble now.

"Where did that thing come from? Is that normal? Are there more out there?"

"Just hang on, son. Give me a moment. Crap, I need more room."

Pete pulled his pack out of the trench. Desperate, frustrated, he dumped everything onto the snow. He found his kit and dressed his arm as best he could. But he didn't have any antibiotics, and he feared his arm would go septic.

Those big cats have all kinds of bacteria growing under their claws. The snow's cold should slow the growth of an infection, though. All the same, this is very bad. How in the hell could I forget antibiotics?

He stuffed everything back into his pack, anxious to get warm. Shaking, he climbed into the shelter and bundled up as best he could.

The candle had blown out so he relit it, trying to get any extra measure of heat he could. Then he lay down, trying to calm his nerves and fix his mind elsewhere, to some place, any place, warm and safe.

"Pete! You've got to tell me what happened out there."

With Travis's broken legs and now Pete's arm, their situation was worse than he wanted to admit.

"That mountain lion spotted me when I was taking a leak."

"How'd you get rid of it?"

"I bashed it on the nose with my pack shovel."

"Wow! How is your arm?"

"Listen, Travis. You're a young man, but old enough to be told the truth. Our situation probably couldn't get much worse. I wish it weren't so, son, honest. I'm hoping I don't go into shock from what that big cat did to me. And in the morning I've got to find the strength to build a snow shelter and figure out a way to signal someone that we're here, assuming they look up here. And I'm hoping our food lasts.

"But the real danger is that that damn cat clawed me on the arm and broke my skin. I don't know if you know anything about big cats, but they have a hell of a lot of germs and bacteria lodged underneath their claws, from all the animal flesh they gouge. So now all those germs are inside my body, ready to deliver a big dose of gangrene or a staph infection. And if that happens, I can kiss my arm good-bye and probably my life."

Even in the dark Pete saw Travis's despair spread across his face like a poison. Travis swept a trembling hand across his eyes.

"And then there's you, poor kid. You didn't break your legs clean. Each one is a compound fracture, which means it broke the skin. I put antiseptic on your legs before I wrapped each one, but it was just topical. If your bloodstream is infected, then you're in real trouble, just like me. We've got to get to a hospital soon.

"I'm sorry if all this information is too much for you right now, but I figured it's better that you know what we're dealing with. So each of us needs to keep wired really, really tight. Do you think you can do that?"

Travis nodded with a zombie-like stare.

Nuts! I overwhelmed him. Poor kid has been through hell, and I steamrolled him with my words.

"I'm sorry, Travis. I went too heavy on you, I know."

"We don't really have a choice, Pete, do we?"

For the first time Pete saw Travis more as a comrade and less as a liability. He was almost asleep when Travis spoke again.

"Pete, are you afraid?"

"A little bit, Travis. I'll be honest, I'm fighting to stay hopeful right now. But from what I know of God, He has a flair for coming through when hope is lost."

"I'm not religious or anything, Pete, but I'm glad you're here with me. I think I'm most afraid of dying alone."

Pete wanted to weep for Travis, to guarantee him that they'd be rescued, to heal him miraculously, to…save him. But he was powerless. All he had was God. A sad, ironic smile crossed his lips. Then the voice in his head, the voice that was not his own, suddenly spoke.

"Strengthen your younger brother, Peter."

But I can't save him, God.

"No, but I can."

The old soldier in Pete somehow knew what to do. He climbed out of his sleeping bag, careful not to hurt his wounded arm further, and crawled to Travis. Kneeling above him, he inched toward his face, searching for Travis's eyes despite the darkness.

"Travis, this old body of mine has been through a lot. A lot. I've been through shit no one should have to go through. And what I've learned of God, He loves to come through in hopeless situations. Do you believe me?"

Pete heard Travis swallow hard. Was he holding back tears?

"Yes, Pete. But…I don't really know why."

"That's okay. Sometimes it's enough just to trust."

"If you say so."

Pete kissed Travis on the forehead, cupping the back of his head as he did so. It was something he'd done with his children and grandchildren all his life. Then he crawled back to his sleeping bag and let welcomed sleep overtake him. He dreamt.

· · ·

Pete was inside a whale, sitting in a small rowboat opposite his old friend David Bates. Each of them was dressed in the olive drab clothing of an American soldier in World War II, wearing a helmet and a weapon slung over the shoulder. They were arguing about how to get out of the whale and onto the beach they were supposed to be on.

"It'll be all right, Pete. Everything's going to work out. Don't worry about it."

"Damn it, Dave! Don't you get it?! We're lost, brother. Totally lost! And I don't need this shit! I'm tired of it. Nothing is working out. Nothing ever seems to work out. Am I supposed to be satisfied sitting in whale blubber?!"

A small-town, homey type of toothy grin was permanently plastered across Dave's face. "It's not so bad, Pete. You're just too demanding, that's all. It all depends on how you look at things, see?"

Pete reached across and held Dave's face firmly in his hands. "No, Dave! You're wrong!"

Then Dave's face changed. It had cuts and wounds all over it, and blood poured out of each one. His mouth was open, but no words came out, and his eyes were wide and vacant. The lower half of Dave's body was missing, and suddenly realizing this, Pete screamed.

Then their little boat rocked and heaved, and they shot out of the whale's mouth like a bullet. They crashed down onto a rocky beach in a heap of shattered wood. Pete stood and brushed himself off. When Pete looked up, he realized they'd landed on the exact beach they were supposed to be on all along.

"There, you see!" exclaimed the bloody half-Dave. "We were on the right course all along, Pete!"

"Yeah, but that doesn't mean I had to enjoy it!"

In the half-light just before dawn, Pete jerked awake. The candle in their shelter had gone out. A gust of wind smacked Pete in the face. David Bates consumed his thoughts.

Geez, I've haven't had a dream that vivid for a long, long time. Not since the years just after the war. What was that all about?

"Hope" was what he heard, almost forgetting he'd asked a question. He felt ashamed, thinking he should've known better.

Anxious to dig a snow cave before the storm he knew was coming, he stumbled out of the shelter. His shovel and skis lay in the snow. He needed to find a hill, even a small one, in order to dig a proper snow cave, one that would offer better protection than the shelter they had at the moment.

There were plenty of hillsides, but all of them were covered with trees, making a snow cave impossible to construct. Discouraged and anxious, he struggled back to the shelter, a whispered stream of desperate prayers escaping his lips.

The return trip seemed to take an hour, though it was only half that long. Pete skied as close to the shelter as he could, then unclipped his bindings and tumbled inside in a heap. He had trouble locating his headlamp, then finally realized he'd rolled on top of it. He turned it on and found his first aid kit. With shaking hands he found some pain reliever and swallowed a double dose. Then he checked the dressing on his arm. It was oozing and needed to be changed, but instead he collapsed to the floor of the snow shelter, too tired to continue. The dressing would have to wait.

Pete fought with himself. *Come on, McGregor! What the hell is wrong with you?! Man, I'm exhausted. I'm not winded; I'm tired deep down.*

Pete was afraid that perhaps one of his greatest fears had come true: the loss of his strength. That he was really just a weak, tired old man.

"What's up, Pete?"

Pete was aware Travis was speaking to him, but responding felt like performing complex math equations—impossible in his current state. Pete's head felt as though it was mounted on a turntable that was spinning round and round. His joints ached, too, along with his head. Unsure how much time had passed since Travis asked him a question, somehow he had the presence of mind to respond.

"I tried to look for an open spot so I could dig out a snow cave for us. But I don't feel too well. I'll try again later. I'm sorry, son. We'll really be much better off in a snow cave. I'll try and build one in a little while. Just give me some time to rest up."

"Okay, Pete, but my legs really hurt. Do you have some more shit I can take to ease the pain?"

"Yeah, sure. Just fish around inside my pack for my first aid kit. There's ibuprofen in there. I'm really not doing too well right now. I need to rest."

Pete heard grunts as Travis reached for Pete's heavy pack and dragged it closer, then rummaged around inside it.

Eyes closed, Pete admonished him, saying, "Use a flashlight, Travis. You don't want to take the wrong kind of medication. There's a small light in one of the side pouches of my pack."

More rummaging, grunting, and zippers opening and closing, interspersed with a "humph" here and there as Travis examined the contents in Pete's backpack.

"Did you find it?" Pete said after several minutes.

"Yeah, but I found some Percocet too. Wouldn't that be better to take?"

Oh hell, he's right. Why didn't I think of that? I am really off my game!

The specters of being old and losing strength danced about the edges of Pete's mind, and he struggled to keep them at bay.

Eyes still closed, Pete said, "Oh, Travis, you're right. I forgot I had that. I'm sorry. Yes, Percocet would be much better for your pain. Besides, it'll keep you buttoned up on your backside, which is a nice benefit."

"Huh?"

"It'll constipate you."

"Oh."

Later that morning Travis's shouting pulled Pete from a dead sleep. He sat up but didn't recognize where he was.

"Pete! Are you okay? You were saying some really weird shit while you were sleeping. Crazy stuff."

Pete felt warm and his body ached a bit. He feared he might have a slight fever. His arm ached dully too. But he felt less tired than the day before. He peered at Travis through the dim light, afraid of what he'd revealed in his sleep.

"What did I say?"

"First you were arguing with someone named Dave, and talking about 'krauts,' or something like that. Then you were apologizing really loudly to some dude named Sarge. You're freaking me out. Who are those guys?"

How do I answer that question? Pete wondered. His wartime experiences were precious to him, even sacred. And he normally revealed them only to those he believed had "earned" it, and even then it was only in the right circumstance.

Well, McGregor, if this poor kid hasn't suffered enough to earn it, then nobody has. Besides, what the heck else is there to do?

"Those are the names of some good men I knew a long time ago. We were in the war together, and they've haunted me ever since."

"You said 'The Big One' earlier. Is that World War II?"

"Yes."

"But if those men you fought with were good, why do they haunt you?"

Images flooded Pete's mind, of comrades in olive drab, their dirty, unshaven faces partially hidden by helmets pressed low on their heads, weapons at the ready and gripped by white-knuckled hands. Of always being tired, cold, and hungry. Of men, young and scared shitless, screaming and bleeding from being shot or hit with shrapnel. And worse, of boys with hopeless eyes, whispering for their mothers as life drained away.

Pete wept. But he didn't weep because of wasted young lives. They weren't a waste. It was a necessary war. Pete had always known this. He wept for the lives cut short, for what might have been, and because he lived while others did not.

Travis's face twisted, a mixture of horror and shame. "Dang it, Pete, I'm sorry. I really am. I didn't mean to barge into your deepest thoughts. Crap! I asked too many questions. I always do this. I'm an idiot. I'm sorry."

Pete's quiet sobs disappeared as quickly as they'd come, like a summer squall in the high mountains. *Lives cut short,* thought Pete.

Too many of those. God, I don't know what You've got planned, but I know You care about Travis. If it's part of Your plan, grant me the grace to keep Travis's life from being cut short too. Amen.

"You're not an idiot, Travis. Far from it. There's no way you could've known that what you said would be hard on me. Why are you being so hard on yourself?"

Travis hung his head. In a whisper he said, "Sorry again. I'm sort of used to hearing how much I screw up. It's routine for me."

"Like a dog that's always being beaten," Pete said.

Travis kept his head down.

Pete was fully awake now and decided to change the dressing on his wounded arm. The gauze was soaked with blood and pus. Pete swallowed another pain reliever and was about to lie down.

"Who was Dave, Pete?"

"Excuse me?"

"Who was Dave? Was he a good friend? Did he die in the war? I know I've asked too many questions about the war but, I dreamt of Zach last night. It was weird. I didn't even know him all that well. But the dream felt so real, Pete. Even when I woke up I wasn't sure…I'm still not sure if it was really just a dream or really him. It's like he is somehow visiting or haunting me, maybe because I got him killed.

"And, well, maybe that's why you always dream of Dave—because he died or something really bad happened to him. And I'm afraid Zach's ghost will torment me the rest of my life. I know that sounds self-centered and makes me look like a jerk. I guess it's just that it's comforting talking to you. You aren't like my dad or my gramps at all. I mean that in a good way."

Pete's belly began churning and his breathing shortened. He felt like Moses encountering the burning bush—about to tread on holy ground. The sudden stillness of the air seemed to press down on his chest. Pete lost track of how long he sat there, speechless.

"Pete? Did you fall asleep?"

"I met David Bates in college. He became my best friend. We went through a lot together. He was one of the few truly good men I think I've ever known. And I managed to kill him."

"Shit," Travis said, barely above a whisper.

3 - FAMILIAR GROUND

The flame of their candle suddenly whipped about as an icy gust of wind whirled around inside the shelter, bringing with it a frosty handful of fresh snow that dusted everything.

"I met David Bates during my first year at CU, in Boulder. I think that must've been about 1937. He was a graduate student, working on his doctorate in engineering. He was a smart cookie.

"Anyway, the war came along and we joined the army's division of the mountain troops. We trained here in Colorado, then went to war in the mountains of Italy. I was one cocky son of a bitch!" Pete exclaimed, shaking his head with a laugh.

Then Pete's face clouded over. Hesitating, he softly said, "But the war certainly changed all that. I survived, but the ghosts that haunted me afterward were the price I had to pay." A sparkle suddenly danced about Pete's eyes. "But the trick is to embrace the ghosts, to realize that God uses them to change you. But only if you let Him. And, well, it's a hard journey, Travis."

Again it was silent in the shelter, and still. Pete felt as though his soul momentarily left his body and hovered somewhere just above his head. Hovering next to him was another presence. It radiated power, but peace too. Even without an exchange of words, somehow Pete could sense the presence telling him that everything would be okay, one way or another. Travis's voice brought him back.

"What have the ghosts told you?" Travis whispered. The tone of his voice suggested regret.

Pete turned to Travis, and for the first time he seemed to catch a glimpse inside him, somewhere behind his eyes. There was a softening in Travis. Or was it brokenness?

"That's a powerful question. I'm not sure you fully realize what you're asking, son. Are you sure you want to know?"

"We're stuck, Pete, right? What the hell else are we going to do? Besides, I need something to take my mind off all this crap."

"I suppose you're right. And there's another storm moving in. I didn't want to tell you, but it wouldn't be fair if I didn't. I'm afraid we'll be here a while."

"Are we going to be okay in this shelter? Didn't you say we need a snow cave?"

"This will have to be enough. I need a hillside free of trees to dig a cave. I couldn't find one earlier, and now there isn't enough time. I'm sorry."

"Do you think they'll find us? I mean, how are they going to see us?"

"They'll keep looking. But with another storm moving in, it'll make the search even more difficult. I'd hoped to be able to guide you out or pull you out, but with everything that's happened…well, I guess I'm too banged up to do that."

"Is it hopeless? Seriously, Pete, are we screwed?"

"Maybe. But we can't lose heart. If you lose heart, you've lost everything."

"But if we are screwed, what's the point of pretending that we aren't?"

Pete dropped his head, pursed his lips, and traced his finger in the packed snow of the shelter's floor. He ran his thin, veiny hand through his even thinner, short, silvery hair. He envisioned his death and his wife, as well as his children and grandchildren, getting the news. He winced at the thought, closing his eyes. Worse, he thought of Travis's death, his parents realizing the deepest fear of any parent: having to bury a child. Fear and faith brawled with each other in his heart. And there it was. The battle Pete had waged his whole life.

I'm afraid, God. I thought my faith was strong, but it seems so weak. I hate that it's such a struggle to trust You. Why am I so weak sometimes?

"You pray for strength, Peter. But I'm always breaking you, making you weak."

Why, God?

"You know why."

Pete knew why. He'd known for most of his life. And he hated that the answers to his deepest questions always came back to the same place.

"My grace is sufficient for you. My strength is perfected in your weakness," Pete whispered.

"What did you say, Pete?"

Pete thought he was done hearing from God, for now. Not quite.

"Tell him your story."

What if it won't make a difference?

"Take the risk, son. Travis matters. All lives matter to Me."

Pete raised his head and leaned in toward Travis, narrowing his eyes and looking him full in the face. Pete could see the deep, childlike fear behind the young man's eyes. He felt small and foolish for not noticing it until now. A voice in his head, not from God and not his own—was it the devil?—tried to accuse him of not being a real man, of being inadequate and having nothing to say. Pete did his best to fight through it, but he felt like lying down and going to sleep. Then something inside seemed to fill his heart, giving him the courage to speak.

Is this Your grace, God?

"I've been doing this a long time, Travis. A long, long time. I've been on so many adventures, I stopped keeping track years ago. And the one certainty I can tell you is that you'll have a better chance of surviving if you keep hope alive, if you refuse to give up, no matter what happens."

Pete leaned in even closer, as though he didn't even want the trees around them to hear. He was certain Travis would see the worry lines around his eyes and at the corners of his mouth. "I don't know if we're going to make it, son. I really don't. Maybe our time is up, maybe it isn't. I hope it isn't. But it's up to God. If you choose to trust me, do what I tell you, and fight to stay hopeful, you just might find the grace to make it through today. Do you believe me?"

Travis stared back with big, unblinking eyes. His mouth hung open, and he seemed to be barely breathing.

"Travis, do you believe me?" Pete whispered.

"W-what about tomorrow, Pete? And the next day? And the day after that?"

"A day at a time, son. That's all I can promise you. We can only take it a day at a time."

"What if…well, what if I trust you and I end up dying? What then?"

"All I can tell you is that if you don't trust me, you will certainly die. You'll have to take a risk if you want to live."

"I'm afraid, Pete."

"You should be. It's okay to be afraid. However, I think it'll help if I tell you my story."

"Your story?" Travis asked, his confusion obvious.

"Yes. Each person's life is a kind of story. There are easy chapters, hard chapters, exciting chapters, and chapters not so exciting. But all of them are important. Together they make up a story. And the story of a person's life will tell you a lot. It will tell you what really matters, about them and, if you're lucky, about yourself."

"I'm still not sure I understand."

"Okay, but I'll tell you my story anyway. I'll be more brief with the boring…well, the less exciting parts. Okay?"

"Okay, Pete, if you think it'll help."

"I was born in 1917, Travis, in Cleveland, Ohio, to a wealthy family," Pete began. "We made our money in shipping. We had freighters all over the Great Lakes," Pete said, chuckling. And suddenly he was back in time, telling his story as he saw it in his mind, just like a movie.

4 - A LONG AND WINDING ROAD

During Pete's senior year in high school, in the fall of 1934 and the spring of 1935, he wasn't sleeping well. He was anxious about his future, but felt he shouldn't have been. He had a nice life, and he had plans, after attending Princeton, to go into his family's shipping business, like his brother, and one day take it over.

But his heart wasn't in it, and he knew it. He tried to convince himself otherwise, but during the night, lying awake in his bed or talking to the moon as he stood in its silver light, he was honest with himself. "I was meant for more than this," he repeatedly told himself. But what was he yearning for? Life as a shipping magnate seemed boring, and Pete feared boredom more than anything.

On a whim, his thoughts full of adventure and romance and the lure of the West, the day after he graduated from high school, before all the celebratory parties and endless thank-you notes to relatives near and distant, Pete slipped out of bed before the early sunrise of late spring. He dressed quickly, raided the refrigerator of meats and cheeses, liberated the bread box of its loaf, filled his dad's flask with gin, and sneaked out to his Model A Ford. He'd secretly packed it the night before, with a couple of suitcases as well as his father's Colt Model 1911 pistol. He backed his car out of the gravel driveway as gently and quietly as he could and headed west, fear and excitement tightening his stomach and making his palms sweat.

Despite getting lost for a time somewhere in the middle of Indiana (all those damn corn rows look the same!), he managed to make it to the rich farm country of southern Illinois by his third day on the road. As best he could tell, he was generally heading in the proper direction of St. Louis.

In midmorning he stopped for gas at a general store somewhere between Pana and Vandalia on Route 51. Two men sat on a bench outside the flimsy front door, with its peeling paint and torn screen. One of the men was black, the other white. The black man was gaunt and seemed to swim in his overalls and dirty flannel shirt, which he seemed comfortable wearing despite the spring heat. The white man was like his opposite: corpulent, with rivers of sweat running down his gravelly beard and chest, despite his thin white T-shirt stretched tight over his rolls of fat. To the left, a mechanic in filthy coveralls was under the hood and bent over the engine of a rusted-out tow truck.

Pete bought a grape Nehi and a package of beer nuts, and made sure he was heading in the right direction toward St. Louis, while an underfed young attendant, probably no more than thirteen or fourteen, his hair slicked back with cream, filled his car with gas.

Pete got back in his car and continued south, feeling a bit uneasy for some reason. His coat lay on the seat beside him. He slid his hand over it, feeling for his dad's pistol tucked inside.

Sometime past noon Pete decided he'd look for a diner to grab lunch, having finished the food he'd brought with him by the end of the second day. There was something in the distance, but the heat from the road made it shimmer and squirm like liquid, and he couldn't yet tell what it was. Moments later he realized it was an overturned car. A big man, bald, was standing next to it, waving his arms frantically.

Pete slowed, then finally came to a stop. The big man, his white shirt untucked and smeared with blood, walked toward Pete's side of the car in a manner that seemed too casual for a man in an emergency. Somewhere in the back of Pete's mind he knew something was odd. The man glared at him. Pete was about to speak, but instead fumbled for his pistol. It was too late. Two more men suddenly appeared next to his passenger door. They were on him before he could scream.

When Pete woke up, it was dark. A cool wind blew across his face, and it felt good. Pete wasn't sure where he was, only that he was lying down on a hard surface. Something was draped across him. Pete thought, *Is that my jacket?* His whole body hurt, but especially his head, which felt like someone was steadily beating a gigantic war drum somewhere behind his eyes. He tried to sit up, but a pair of hands pushed him back down.

"Whoa, easy there, young squire," came a nearby voice, which fouled the air above his face with the stench of hard liquor. "You're a mess, kid. So just stay still and rest a bit."

"Where the hell am I?"

"You're on the side of the road, just north of Vandalia, to be precise."

Suddenly Pete remembered where he was. Panic filled his heart. "My car! Where's my car?" He sat up, and everything around him felt like a carousel on high speed. His stomach somersaulted, and he barely had time to turn his head and vomit. Afraid he'd look weak and foolish, he scrambled to his feet, wiping pieces of vomit from his lips. His legs felt like liquid, and he collapsed, hitting the hard ground.

"Damn it, kid, I told you to stay put and rest a bit! What the hell is wrong with you?"

Pete's eyes darted back and forth, and finally he found the face of the voice talking to him. It was a round face, outlined by a growth of beard that was evident even in the dark. The stranger wore something that looked like a fedora that had seen better days, with twig-like strands of hair poking out around his ears.

"My car," Pete said. "How's my car?"

The stranger laughed for a moment. "I'm not sure it can be defined as a 'car' any longer. It's up on blocks and the wheels are gone; same with parts of the body. They probably did the same with the engine."

Those bastards! Pete thought. "Why me?" was all he managed to say.

"It ain't you per se, kid. These thugs are real pros. They fake a car accident, get some poor do-gooder to stop, then they're on 'em like flies on a rib roast. They take whatever they think they can barter or sell, which is usually a lot these days."

Pete felt stupid and naïve, and cursed himself for being snookered, as well as for not having his pistol handy. *Oh crap!* He realized his coat had been draped across him, like a blanket, and now he frantically searched its pockets. His dad's pistol was gone. Even more panicked now, he searched the secret pocket in the lining of his coat. Whew! His stash of money was still there.

"Who are you?" Pete said.

"Name's Louis, Louis Kelly. Everyone just calls me Kelly," he said, thrusting a powerful, beefy hand from the frayed sleeve of a dull-gray herringbone overcoat. Odors of gin and sweat swept over Pete like a thick cloud.

"Can you help me up?"

Kelly's firm hand gingerly helped Pete to his feet, holding his shoulders to steady him. Kelly's stench was even more powerful now, and Pete tried hard to hold down another bout of vomit. He succeeded until he got to his car, then blew chunks near the rear fender.

His insides felt somewhat better, enough so that he realized one of his eyes was slightly swollen and tender to the touch. His ribs hurt, too, and sharp pains shot through his right hip every time he took a step.

Pete searched his car for his suitcases. They were gone. All he had now were the clothes he wore, his canvas coat, and his secret stash of money tucked inside it.

Pete needed a place to rest for the night. Kelly led him to a hobo camp a few miles away. He dined on a makeshift stew of muskrat, onions, and turnips, with a small hunk of dark, stale bread. There were about a dozen little camps within the confines of the entire camp, each one marked by a small fire pit scraped out of the hard dirt. Pete ate while sitting in the dirt near the fire of Kelly's camp, which consisted of an old, burning tire. Pete had to get up, painfully, every now and then as the wind shifted direction, to avoid being engulfed by the foul, oily smoke the tire gave off. He tried to assess the men sitting nearby while avoiding eye contact.

One of the men, who was called Bags, talked nonstop, competing with Kelly for attention. He was powerfully built, his barrel chest and bulky shoulders bulging through his faded, buttoned-up shirt and denim jacket. Another one, named Vollmer, appeared to be the smart aleck of the group, able to make dry, witty remarks at will about almost anything. His dark hair was short and bristly, and his overcoat was two sizes too big, engulfing his compact body. Finally, other than Kelly, there was the camp cook, Spikes. He was called this because of something about playing baseball in the big leagues and for a short time being as fast as Billy Sunday, until his knee gave way. His big nose dominated his thin face and close-set eyes. He was wiry, which Pete thought strange for someone always around food (what little there was).

Each man had his own pup tent, and Kelly made room for Pete within his. There was no actual floor to the tent, but Kelly spread a moth-eaten, grimy wool blanket on the crusty ground for Pete to sleep on. Pete buried himself beneath his coat. Despite his pain, sheer exhaustion pulled Pete into a deep sleep quickly.

A warm wind and the smell of burning rubber woke Pete. It felt as though every muscle in his body ached, even his eyelids. He struggled to sit up. He was alone in the tent. He threw off his coat and staggered out of the tent like an old, arthritic man.

The tire was still burning, but the flames were much smaller. The washed-out sky hurt Pete's eyes when he looked up at it. He scanned the camp from where he stood, looking for Kelly, desperate for something to eat. His stomach felt like it was being sucked in toward his backbone, as though it would disappear from the gnaw of hunger.

Suddenly Pete's thoughts were interrupted by the banging of metal on metal and the high squeal of steel wheels. *That's it!* thought Pete. *I'll hitch my way to St. Louis, find the train station, and buy a ticket on an express train to Denver. Blue skies, mountains, snow, dry air. It'll be perfect.*

"Whatchya thinkin' 'bout, Pete?"

It was Kelly, standing nearby with a paper bag in his hand and a crooked smile on his face. Pete's eyes had been closed, and he hadn't heard him approach.

"I need to get to St. Louis so I can hop a train to Denver. I'm trying to make it out west."

"Oh, okay. You're pretty banged up, though. Are you sure you don't want to rest here for a few days?"

"No, Kelly, but thanks. I really need to move on."

"Well, I got some stale rolls and doughnuts here in this bag. Why don't you take a few?"

Pete thanked him and reached in the bag. He grabbed a crusty roll and a glazed doughnut. But before he could leave, Kelly reached in the bag, grabbed a roll and doughnut for himself, then gave the rest of the bag to Pete. Slowly he accepted it but grew suspicious and tried to hand it back. Kelly refused.

"Ah, go on and take it, Petey! I'm a man of the cloth, see? Well, that's not exactly true. I used to be, until my wife left me." Kelly's eyes were suddenly rimmed with tears, and his voice dropped. "Then I turned to John Barleycorn and lost my flock as well." He said nothing more, lowering his head, seemingly lost in thought. Then he perked up as if a switch had been flipped. "But God has never left me!" he asserted, swaying slightly as he pointed his finger skyward. He still smelled like gin.

Later in the morning Pete limped into the town of Vandalia, dragging his aching body over the debris and weeds that lined Route 51. He felt as though the sun was baking his shadow into the dirt. His sweat mixed with the dust that coated his face, creating brown streaks that ran down his cheeks. His coat, draped over his arm, burdened him, and he longed to discard it but knew better. He was grateful for the striped awnings of the businesses on the main road through town, slowing his pace in their shade. He stopped in Belle's Blue Plate for breakfast, across the street from the Hotel Evans and the Ford dealership owned by What's-His-Name & Sons.

In the diner the black-and-white tiled floor gave off a faint scent of bleach that mixed peculiarly with the smells of coffee and bacon and the sweet fragrance of smoke from an elderly man's pipe. Though the start of the day was long past, the five swivel chairs at the red-topped counter were all occupied by men hunkered down eating breakfast or nursing a cup of coffee. One of the four booths was empty, along with two of the four tabletops. The customers at the booths and tables stared at Pete when he entered. His face grew hot, his eyes locked onto the empty booth, and he slid into it as quickly and inconspicuously as he could.

A hefty, older waitress in a pink uniform, with silvery hair held in place by a hairnet, slapped a menu down on the table. "Coffee?" she asked, and produced a cup which she began to fill before Pete could reply. Steam curled up from the black liquid. Pete mumbled something about cream and sugar. All the waitress said in response was "Table," and she tilted her head toward Pete's table, then walked away to attend to the other customers. Pete turned. Hidden behind bottles of ketchup and mustard were a glass jar half-filled with sugar and a small, ceramic container of cream packets. He prepared his coffee, and though it was hot outside, the hot liquid soothed his dry throat.

Suddenly Pete realized that his hunger seemed to be eating away his stomach. He ordered a mound of hash browns, scrambled eggs, toast, and orange juice.

When the waitress brought his food a short time later, he asked, "Ma'am, do you always have so many customers this late in the morning?"

She stared at him as though she didn't understand English. Then her eyes narrowed and she said, "Ain't hardly nobody working these days, young man. Been like this everywhere, for a long time. You been livin' in a cave or something?"

She let out a sigh of bewilderment (or was it disgust?), walking off before Pete could reply. He felt foolish but was too hungry to dwell on it. He plowed into his food, pausing between bites now and then to take a sip or a breath.

When Pete finished his meal and the waitress brought the check, he asked, "Ma'am, will that road out there take me to St. Louis?" He pointed in the direction of the main intersection in Vandalia.

The waitress raised a penciled-in eyebrow. "Of course, honey, if you mean Route 40. Looky here," she said, holding up her palm and using it as a map. "The road right outside is Route 51; it runs north and south. The road you want is the one that bisects it, in the main intersection in town. That's Route 40. It'll take you directly into St. Louis. Got it?"

Pete was pretty sure he wouldn't have a problem making it to St. Louis, but something in his eyes must have said otherwise, as the waitress looked at him suspiciously. "You got a car, son? You look to be a little wet behind the ears to own an automobile. How you plan on gettin' there?"

"I figured I'd just hitch a ride or hop on a freight train," Pete said, doing his best to sound as nonchalant as possible. He fiddled with his spoon.

Something in the older woman's face softened. "Oh hell, child, just wait a minute. You shouldn't be hitching rides in these parts nowadays, especially not as you get closer to St. Louis." Her eyes scanned the diner as she spoke. Suddenly she fixed her gaze on something across the room. "Billy! Ain't you heading into St. Louis today?"

"Yeah, just as soon as I stop by the feed store!" Billy shouted in response. "Why?"

"This young man here needs a lift there. You mind taking him along?"

"Not at all, if he don't mind goin' to the feed store first."

Pete's face flushed hot. He felt exposed. But he was too grateful for the ride to argue. A few minutes later he found himself riding shotgun on a worn, torn seat in the cab of a Chevy pickup truck that had been new in the early part of the Roaring Twenties. Dust covered the dashboard, and coarse planks covered the flatbed in the back. It was impossible to determine what the truck's original paint color had been.

"Billy," the owner of the truck said, introducing himself while clenching a corn cob pipe in his yellow teeth. He wore striped overalls, and his frayed straw hat sat toward the back of his head. Sweat stains darkened the armpits of his flannel shirt, which had been converted (without any particular attention to precision) into a short-sleeved shirt. The heels of Billy's tobacco cowboy boots were almost worn flat. His thick belly strained the straps of his overalls, and Pete wondered if the clasps might give way at any moment. Every few minutes Billy reached into his pocket, pulled out a faded red handkerchief, and blew his nose in a way that sounded like someone stepping on a goose.

When they got to the feed store, Pete waited in the cab, engine running, while Billy hustled inside. The expansive store, made of bleached-out clapboards devoid of paint, thrust itself into the blue sky in a sad kind of way, as though the building was attempting to hang on to its glory from previous decades. A few minutes later a mountain of a man trundled out, holding a feed sack on each shoulder, while Billy trailed behind. He plopped them onto the bed of the truck, and Billy waited nearby while the towering store hand retrieved two more sacks.

While he was waiting, Billy reached into the front pocket of his overalls, pulled out a small sack of tobacco, and stuffed a wad into his pipe. Then he tamped it down, stuffed in another wad, and tamped this down as well. He did this one more time, then struck a match, lit the bowl of his pipe, and blew thick drafts of sweet-smelling smoke into the air. Some of it drifted into the cab of the truck. Pete didn't mind too much; it smelled good.

The store hand returned and threw the sacks into the bed of Billy's truck. Billy paid him, hopped in the cab, ground the gear shift into first, and the truck lurched out of the feed store parking lot, heading for Route 40 west to St. Louis.

Pete clenched his coat, which lay in his lap, as the truck bounced down the dirt highway, windows down and the wind whipping through the cab. Billy mumbled something, but the noise from the wind made it impossible for Pete to comprehend what he'd said. Pete just smiled and nodded. Billy cocked his head as he looked at Pete—in between glancing at the road—in such a way that Pete knew Billy expected a response that involved actual words. Pete's face grew hot.

Suddenly more uncomfortable than he already was, Pete blurted out, "What did you say, Billy?"

Billy held up his index finger, then rolled up his window halfway and indicated for Pete to do the same. Now it was easier to hear.

"I said, 'Why ya heading to St. Louis?' Ya lookin' for a job?"

"No. I'm catching a train out west, to Denver."

"Ah, I see. Ya gotta girl out there, do ya?"

Pete felt somewhat insulted, for some reason, as though going to such great lengths for a woman was somehow undignified. "No, not at all, Billy. I'm going out west for some adventure, to make my fortune, you might say."

Billy laughed out loud, from his considerable belly, which turned into him blowing his nose with his kerchief. "I'm sorry, son. I don't mean to insult you or anything. It's just that the gold and silver rush in Colorado ended about forty years ago."

"Yeah, yeah, I know that," Pete said quickly. But he only vaguely remembered it from a high school history lesson. "I don't mean that kind of fortune."

Billy stroked his chin. "I wasn't aware there's more than one kind of 'fortune.'"

Pete turned and watched the spring wind whip across fields of newly planted crops. The sun seemed to ricochet off the leaves in the trees that were transitioning from the tender green of spring to the deeper, mature green of summer. "I meant that I'm looking for adventure."

"Oh, I see. Well, there's plenty of adventure in the mountains, kid." Billy had finished his pipe. He dumped the remaining ashes out the window, then proceeded to fill his pipe for another round. "Pete, can you steer for me while I fill my pipe?"

Pete grabbed the wheel with his left hand, only then realizing how bald the tires on Billy's truck were. It steered like a sponge, and Pete jerked the worn steering wheel back and forth to try to hold the truck to something resembling a straight line. The front wheels skidded left and right over the dirt anyway.

Billy finished filling his pipe and somehow managed to get it lit despite the constant wind. Then he thanked Pete and grabbed the steering wheel.

"So what kind of adventure are you lookin' for?"

"I'm not sure. Any kind, I guess."

Billy got a faraway look in his eyes as though he was trying to see something on the horizon. "Just remember that jobs is hard to come by. So don't limit yourself. Look everywhere. Now let's see, what could you do?" Billy wondered aloud before disgorging a milky white cloud of tobacco smoke, the size of a baseball, from his mouth. "You could try to get on with the Denver and Rio Grande West, but jobs with the railroad is next to impossible to get, unless you know someone. And from the looks of ya, I can only assume that don't apply to you. Some of the mines from the old days are still in operation, but just barely. You might have better luck finding work on a ranch or maybe with the CCC. Those government boys are always up in the mountains building this or clearing that."

"How do you know so much about Denver, Billy?"

Something came over Billy, and he said nothing for a long time. The wind, hot now, whistled through the cab and carried the white, marbled smoke from his pipe out over the countryside. Pete wondered if he'd offended him or if perhaps Billy had a dark past he wanted to keep hidden.

"I worked in the Lebanon silver mine, in Georgetown, Colorado, beginning in the mid-80s. My older brother, Henry, did too. We was orphans. Our mom died from consumption—that's what they called tuberculosis back then—and our dad was killed a year or so later, in a saloon fight. We was just kids when we started working, but that's how them Cornish miners liked it. It was dangerous work, but we got paid well. We ran supplies up to the mine and kept the stove going in camp, which the miners used to dry their clothes.

"Everything was going well, but one day, in the winter, Henry let the fire go out in the stove. And the miners had a rule that whoever let the fire in the stove go out would get dunked in a rain barrel, because if you let the stove go out, the miners would have to walk home in wet clothes. And if they were forced to do so, they'd force you to do the same. So Henry had to walk home in wet clothes, but we'd been hit with a cold spell at the time." Billy suddenly stopped talking. Then he blew his nose and continued.

"Henry got pneumonia…and the poor kid just never recovered. He was fourteen at the time." Pete turned to look at Billy. Light glinted off his moist eyes. His mouth hung open in a strange way, as though he was about to vomit. "I've thought about my brother every day of my life, Pete. I was all alone after that. Even being married, I felt alone."

Part of Pete envied Billy, for having the freedom to do whatever he wanted. But mostly he felt sad for him, picturing Billy as a small boy and having to fend for himself. A lump grew in his throat, and he blinked his eyes repeatedly to keep tears from forming. Pete's mother had always told him that he was "sensitive," and being a boy, he always feared it might be true.

"But there was plenty of good times too. And as you can see, I'm still here!" Billy said triumphantly. "Hey, ya never told me where you was from, son."

"I'm from the Great Lakes area. Cleveland, to be exact."

"Hell, son, you's a long way from your folks. I'm guessing you ain't even out of yer teens. You gotta be careful nowadays. There's lots of bandits out on the highways. Why ain't ya stayin' put with yer family? Is yer ma and pa still alive?"

"Yeah, Billy, they're still very much alive. But I left home right after I graduated from high school."

"Was yer folks okay with that?"

Pete hesitated just for a moment, but it was long enough for Billy to notice. "They didn't seem to mind."

"Living like the Lone Ranger ain't no way to go through life, son."

"But you've been on your own since you were twelve, Billy. I'm eighteen."

Billy suddenly pulled to the side of the road and skidded to a stop. Pete gripped his coat tighter with one hand and stroked the door handle with the other.

"Listen to me, son," Billy said earnestly. He stared into Pete's eyes, and normally Pete would've recoiled, but there was something comforting in the nearness of Billy's rough, punchy face. Only later did Pete realize that although Billy hardly knew him, he felt like the kind of father Pete had always longed for but never had.

"I was on my own, but only because I had no other choice. I don't wish for no man to have to travel the path I did. It's okay now, and I've always felt that God was with me, watching over me and such. But I paid a high price for it. I been married and divorced three times. I turned to the bottle, and damned if I didn't lose a lot of years because of it. That's why I smoke this pipe, so's I stay away from the bottle, if ya know what I mean. And there's an awful lot of lonely times. No woman, no brother, no ma and pa. Just me. When you get on that train and head out west, you might do best to think about some of the things I'm tryin' to tell ya. Don't be like me, boy." Billy didn't need to add those final words. Pete saw him pleading with his eyes.

The truck's idling engine was the only sound now. Then Billy turned away, gunned the engine, and pulled back onto the highway. Pete's thoughts swirled like a cyclone, thinking about Billy's words, his face, and trying to imagine him as a kid in the Wild West days, wondering about gunfights and the Indian Wars. Then before he knew it, they pulled up to the enormous Union Station. To Pete it looked like a castle.

Billy reached into his back pocket and took out a small roll of bills wrapped with a rubber band. It was all Billy had for a wallet. He handed Pete a five-dollar bill.

"Here you go, Pete. It's all I can spare. I wish it was more," Billy said, a sad smile on his face.

"It's okay, Billy. You don't have to give me that. Really. I still have some money left."

"Go on, kid, just take it. I ain't got no family, remember? And for some reason God wanted us to cross paths. I think He wants me to help take care of you, even if it's only in a small way. I think that's how God works. It's like He ain't gonna do nothin' unless somebody is willing to let Him. Anyway, that's how I see it."

Pete took the bill but found it difficult to look Billy in the eye, even as he thanked him. He slipped it inside his pants pocket as quickly as he could. Then he opened the door of the truck, slid out, and thanked Billy again, only briefly catching his eye as shame washed over him again.

"Well, son, I guess I'll see ya in the funny papers. You remember what I said, will ya? Don't be no Lone Ranger. You let yer ma and pa know how yer doing. They's worried sick about ya, I'm sure."

"Okay, Billy. Maybe you're right."

"Course I'm right!"

Pete watched Billy drive away, determined to catch a train out west, but not too certain about contacting his parents. Slowly he walked through the doors of Union Station, like a log adrift in a fast current.

Though it was the afternoon, the station buzzed with activity like the pits at the Indy 500. It seemed like the whole world was either wearing a trench coat or had one draped over an arm. A shoe shine stand was full, two men waiting in chairs while a boy in a smudged white shirt and herringbone cap attacked the shoes of a third with a cloth. Two newsboys, working for rival papers, sold copies of the afternoon's edition. A young, attractive woman worked a small stand selling cigarettes, candy, gum, and copies of *Life* and *Look*. Two men stood nearby, one slightly bent over, lighting his cigarette from that of the man next to him. Three boys, trailing their parents and dressed in knickers and sweater vests, argued passionately about the current state of the St. Louis Cardinals.

Beams of sunlight shot down from the high glass ceiling to the marble floor in thick shafts that striped the hazy, afternoon air. Pete walked to the ticket booths at the far end of the interior, alternately bathed in sunlight one moment then shadows the next. He purchased a one-way, second-class ticket to Denver aboard the Santa Fe Chief.

5 - TWISTING IN THE WIND

Pete was shaken from his sleep.

"Pete! Pete, wake up! The roof of our shelter is torn or something. It keeps flapping around, and snow is blowing in like crazy."

"What?" Pete said, sitting up, speaking without realizing where he was or what was happening. It took him a few moments to get his bearings.

"The tarp, Pete. The tarp's all jacked up. It's flapping around, and snow is blowing in like crazy, see? I think the storm is here."

"Yeah, okay. What time is it?" Pete ran his hands over his face, trying to rouse himself. The inside of his head pounded like a war drum.

"About five o' clock."

"In the morning or evening?"

"The evening, Pete! Dang, you haven't been asleep that long."

"Right, right. Okay. I probably just need to secure the tarp a little better."

As Pete crawled outside, the snow was blowing sideways, pelting his head and stinging his ears. He worked his way toward the loose flap, sinking into the deep snow all the way to his hip with each step. He tied the loosened anchor, then realized he'd forgotten to place a support pole beneath the center of the tarp to keep the snow from building up on the shelter roof. His headache and the injuries to his arm and back clouded his thoughts. All he could think about was shelter and the warmth of his sleeping bag.

Later, sometime in the night, Pete got up to urinate. The storm was still raging, and he felt no better. But he was dangerously dehydrated, and knew it. After doing his best to relieve himself—while stepping through deep snow without snowshoes—he forced himself to drink an entire liter of water, and felt marginally better. He forced Travis to drink more water as well. Then, while he was in the midst of developing an emergency plan checklist in his head should their situation get worse, sleep overtook him again.

Pete wasn't sure what time it was when he woke up next, only that it was morning. A gray shaft of light penetrated their shelter. Enough snow had fallen that their entrance was almost completely covered up. Pete wiggled out of his bag and crawled to the entrance, where he pushed away piles of new snow. It was still falling from the sky, soft and chunky, but the wind had quit.

Back inside the shelter Pete lit another candle. He was hungry and welcomed the notion of firing up his pack stove to make a hot breakfast.

Maybe I'm getting better.

Without antibiotics, this was merely wishful thinking. He unwrapped his dressing. A faint, pinkish streak had formed. *Damn it!* Pete did his best to tamp down his fear, but his fear of gangrene lingered. He applied more antibiotic cream and slapped on a fresh swath of gauze.

Then he turned on his portable stove. He decided he'd use some of their drinking water to cook with, rather than packing a pot with snow and waiting for it to melt and boil. There'd be plenty of time to melt snow, for drinking, while they ate.

Pete and Travis feasted on Styrofoam cups of steaming, prepackaged corn chowder, with a side of string cheese and trail mix. Pete even used the remaining water to make a cup of instant coffee. He wished he hadn't spilled all the rum.

"Travis, just in case things get worse, we need to have an emergency plan."

"How could things get any worse?"

"You just never know. It happens more than you'd think. It's best to be prepared."

"Okay, if you say so."

"Good. So here's what I'm thinking. If my infected arm gets really bad and I can't haul you out of here, and we still haven't been found, then you're going to inject me with some morphine."

"Geez, how'd you get that kind of stuff?"

"I have some old glass vials of it, from the war. I keep them in a little case, along with a couple of syringes, in a secret compartment inside my pack.

"But there's something else. I have some fire paste in my pack, in a tube that sort of looks like toothpaste. If we're at the end of our rope, and it looks like we aren't going to make it, then I'll take this paste and my Zippo lighter, and crawl to an uphill tree, a safe distance away. I'll take the paste, the whole tube, and smear it as high up on the trunk as I can, as close to the branches as possible. Then I'll light it and get the hell away from it."

"Shit. You're going to deliberately start a forest fire?"

"It's really just a type of emergency flare."

"But what if this whole forest goes up in flames, Pete?"

"It's winter, Travis. Forest fires don't usually occur in winter. There's too much snow. And even if we started one, it would most likely take a long time before we were in danger. We'd be rescued by then, probably. And we're in a snow pit. We're surrounded by frozen water. So it'll be okay. Got it?"

"Do you have some morphine for me too?"

"Yes. Remember, the morphine will only ease the pain while we die."

It was quiet. But the echo of Pete's words violated the stillness with a brutish finality. Fat flakes of snow continued to fall outside the shelter, and the smell of corn chowder and coffee mixed with wet down and old, worn canvas.

"I'm really scared now, Pete."

Even in the weak light of the shelter, Pete saw Travis trembling, and he looked like a child. Pete thought of his own children when they were very young. He wanted to comfort Travis, but suddenly exhaustion and nausea seized him.

I'm in way over my head, he thought. *Can I still do this? I'm tired of the pain. I just want it to end, Lord. I'm overwhelmed, and I feel abandoned by You. I can't help this kid.*

"Go comfort him," said God.

I'm so tired.

"I know you are. Take a step, son. Just take a step. Trust Me."

Okay, Lord, okay.

Pete rose to his knees. Everything started spinning, and Pete braced himself against the snowy wall of the shelter. Then the feeling passed, and Pete crawled to Travis. He cradled the young man's head against his chest.

Travis sobbed. Pete sobbed with him.

6 - WAY OUT WEST

When Pete purchased his train ticket aboard the Santa Fe Chief, the ticketing agent neglected to mention that all the cabins had already been purchased. He boarded the idling, steaming train and wandered around for a while, unsure where his cabin was located. It was then that he asked the conductor, who tersely informed him that, not only was Pete not remotely properly attired, but all the cabins had been purchased. He examined Pete's ticket and pointed to where the fine print clearly stated that Pete's ticket was only good for general passage and, thus, he'd have to spend his nights in either the club car or the dining car.

Pete wandered into the club car to kill time before dinner. Several passengers relaxed in efficient, cloth-covered lounge chairs separated every few feet by narrow oak stands topped with tiny electric lamps that, even in daytime, gave the car a dull, amber glow. Hunter green carpet and a rich, polished cherry wood bar reminded Pete of privileged times, growing up in wealth. But even during those best moments long ago, there always seemed to be something missing, and only now could Pete begin to describe it.

He longed for more, but not more money or possessions. He wanted to be seen, to be cherished, to know that he was delighted in and welcomed. He wanted to know that he mattered, that he was part of something important, and not merely marking time on Earth, waiting to die or looking for the next thrill.

He sat down at the tiny bar, ordered a Tom Collins, and knowingly glanced at the liquor bottles, some of which were his parents' favorites: Johnnie Walker Red, Tanqueray, Stolichnaya, and Dewar's. But it felt as though he was being mocked. It was as if each bottle of alcohol was a reminder that his parents loved the idea of parenting more than the actual task. They enjoyed a good party and fine things, sure, but most of all they enjoyed being the center of the universe, avoiding the messiness of life, and not being inconvenienced too much by the needs of a child.

The bartender was an elderly, balding black man in a crisp, short-waisted green jacket that matched the color of the carpet and was trimmed with gold piping. His red bow tie was like a contrasting punctuation mark to the subdued colors of the club car.

Wow, thought Pete, *the Santa Fe railroad is some kind of swell operation. Even the barkeep looks like a million bucks.*

The barman set a white napkin on the dark, cherry wood counter and gently placed Pete's drink upon it. Pete chugged a third of the sweet, pearly-white concoction, then, feeling self-conscious and unsophisticated, abruptly stopped and casually placed the glass back on the counter, hoping the other patrons hadn't noticed.

Then the club car gave a jolt, lurched forward half a dozen feet, stopped, then gave another jolt and slowly rolled forward. Pete was glad for the diversion from his embarrassment at acting like an uncouth barbarian.

Here's to a new life out west, he thought, subtly hoisting his drink to his lips, careful only to take a sip, then setting it back down.

Fifteen minutes later, with The Chief steadily rolling toward the outskirts of St. Louis, Pete ordered another Tom Collins. It was then that he noticed a tall man enter the club car, his dark hair slicked back, wearing a cream-colored suit across his broad shoulders, a bright blue ascot seemingly tied too tightly around his neck, with a matching pocket kerchief. Everyone seated in the car, especially the women, immediately noticed him. The man was headed straight toward Pete, though he gazed in another direction.

Ah crap! Pete thought. *Please don't sit next to me, please don't sit next to me, please don't sit next to me.* But he shouldn't have been surprised, as he was sitting in the middle of the three bar stools present at the tiny counter.

Sure enough, the man sat right next to Pete. He pulled out a silver cigarette case, retrieved a cigarette, tapped it on the bar, and expertly lit it with a matching silver Zippo lighter, which he quickly snapped shut and slid onto the bar.

"Good evening, Mr. Khouri," the bartender said. "Heading back to Denver so soon?"

"Hello, Moses. Yes, back out west. Duty calls," he responded, rolling his eyes.

"Well, it's nice to see you again, sir. The usual? Double bourbon?"

"Not tonight, Moses. Let's mix it up. How 'bout a vodka tonic?"

"That's a good choice, Mr. Khouri, on a hot day like today. I guess summer is coming early."

Within seconds the barkeep placed Khouri's drink before him, who then slid a generous tip into the man's rough hand. The bartender gave a quick bow of appreciation, then retrieved a clean bar rag and went about wiping down the already gleaming bar top.

Khouri sipped his drink, took a long drag of his cigarette, and blew an enormous cloud of bluish-gray smoke from his nose over the bar. "First time on a train?" he said, without turning his head.

Pete thought maybe he was talking to someone else, so he shot a quick glance toward the stranger, then over his shoulder. No one nearby—just him and the thin, exotic man.

"Well, yeah." The words stumbled from Pete's lips. "How'd you know?"

The dark man smiled but still hadn't looked at Pete. He took another long drag on his cigarette.

Pete's eyes flashed, and his face grew hot.

Staring straight ahead, Khouri tapped some ash into an enameled tray embossed with the logo of the Santa Fe Railroad, leaned toward Pete, and whispered, "It's okay, son. I won't say a word." Then he faced

Pete for the first time and winked. "You better slow down on the spirits, son, otherwise we'll be carrying you out of here. You should have a chaser with your drink. Is that a Tom Collins?"

Pete nodded, speechless, clearly aware he was way out of his league. The stranger made him nervous but intrigued him at the same time.

"Moses, would you be so kind as to bring this young man a Falstaff? Just put it on my tab."

"Of course, Mr. Khouri."

The crazy thing, Pete realized as the beer was poured into a tall, frosted glass before him, was that he couldn't even remember finishing his second mixed drink.

"Oh, and would you mind bringing some sandwiches over? Whatever you have available will be fine, I'm sure."

The thin man abruptly extended one of his large hands toward Pete. "Georges Khouri," he said, while taking a quick puff on his cigarette using his left hand. "And you are?"

"Pete. Peter McGregor."

"Nice to meet you, Pete. My apologies if I came across a bit imperious. Sometimes I get a bit overbearing in, shall I say, adventurous situations."

"Nice to meet you as well," Pete responded automatically, only then wondering if he meant it. "Are you American? You don't sound American."

Khouri let out a laugh, crushed out the remnants of his cigarette, drained half of his drink, and lit another smoke. "Ah, perhaps you catch on quicker than most. I am actually a French citizen, though I was born within the Ottoman Empire, in a tiny region called Lebanon."

Pete wondered if the stranger was playing games. *But,* he thought, *as long as he's paying for the drinks and the food, better to play along just in case.*

"I've never heard of it."

"Of course you haven't," Khouri said somewhat defiantly. "Lebanon isn't even a country. As I said, it's merely a region, part of Syria now, which is a country in the eastern half of the Mediterranean."

"Then how come you're a French citizen?"

Khouri took another drag, narrowed his eyes, and smiled again through the smoke. "You are very perceptive, Peter. I am a French citizen because Syria is a French protectorate. My first language was Arabic, but I know French, too, because Catholic missionaries from France were my instructors in school."

"How did you learn English?"

The dark man finished the remnants of his drink and ordered another round as a waiter, in a white jacket and black bow tie, placed before him and Pete the sandwiches he'd ordered.

"I did well in school, and I earned a scholarship to study at Cambridge. It was a good thing, too, because my family was much too poor to send me to university. But this is all boring history.

"Explain yourself to me. Either you are attending an institute of higher learning, or, from the way you are dressed, you are more likely looking for a new life in, as you Americans say, the Wild West. So which is it?"

Afraid that he seemed so easily exposed, Pete tried to steer the conversation down a tangent. "I've only read about the West, never been there. What is it really like? Is Denver a nice place?"

Khouri didn't respond for a long time—or so it seemed to Pete— and narrowed his eyes while he rested his chin in the hand that held his cigarette, its smoke silently rising less than an inch from his face, curling into a tiny knot just above his hair. Pete fumbled for a sandwich.

"You are dodging my question, Peter. We only dodge questions that make us uncomfortable. If you were going to college, you'd have no reason to be uncomfortable. Thus, logically you must be trying to begin a new life. So why are you seeking a new life? What are you running from?"

Khouri lifted his head from his hand and stared at the ceiling, trying to answer his own question. Pete chewed his sandwich and took a big gulp of his beer. His eyes ping-ponged back and forth between Khouri and others in the club car.

Khouri continued. "You might be running from the law. That's certainly a possibility at your age, but not a probability."

Pete was sweating now, and he nearly drained the rest of his beer. He'd never met anyone so clever, not even the high-priced lawyers of his father's company.

"Either you are running from a lover who broke your heart, or you are running from your parents. So which is it?"

Pete picked up his beer for another sip and only then noticed he was shaking. He felt as though the Middle Easterner had hypnotized him. He wanted to look away, to run from the club car, anything to escape his discomfort! But he couldn't, try as he might.

Nearly trance-like, he mumbled, "M-my parents. I...I can't live with them anymore."

"And why is that?"

Pete couldn't answer. He thought that anything he said next would sound pathetic, childish. *What the hell is wrong with me? I must sound like a drooling buffoon.*

"Are you okay, Peter? You look like you're about to go before a firing squad. Is it my questioning that's upsetting you?"

7 - ALONE TOGETHER

It was night, and Pete did his best to answer Travis's questions, the kind that only come in youth. He cooked them another simple meal. Their provisions were already running low. There was only enough for a few more meals. They still had plenty of water, though Pete had to nag Travis to keep drinking. Then he'd pack more snow into Travis's water bottle and remind him to stash it inside his sleeping bag or some other warm place.

Pete checked his arm. Even in the pale glare of his headlamp, it was clear the infection was spreading. He changed the dressing. The wound itself was just beginning to heal, but the streaks of red, beneath his skin, were darker and longer. And Pete knew he was in trouble.

"How is your arm, Pete?"

"It's bad, Travis. Infection is spreading."

Travis dragged the back of his hand across his forehead. Avoiding Pete's eyes, he asked, "Will you die from it?"

"I'm afraid so, son. My blood is getting infected, and that'll kill me unless we get to a hospital sometime soon."

Neither man spoke. The wind picked up, dusting both men and their gear in a thin, frosty coating of cold, dry snow. Travis's face glistened in the wavering candlelight.

"Are you afraid to die, Pete?" Travis whispered, head down now, his finger tracing a pattern in the floor of packed snow.

Something in his heart told Pete it would be irreverent to answer Travis's question too soon. So he let the question hang in the cold, dense air, unsure when or how he would answer it. To his surprise, Travis said nothing either.

"I'm not afraid to die, Travis. If it's my time to go, so be it. But I'm afraid of the pain for those I love and will leave behind for now," Pete said, staring into the candle's flame. Then he suddenly looked up, as if waking from a dream. "But when I was younger, I felt the opposite way. I was afraid to die because I had so much living to do. This doesn't sound too bad, right? It's the desire of a person who yearns for more, which is good in and of itself. But for me it was self-centered. I lived an existence where I was the center of the universe. However, that's not how life works, see? Life is too big for me or you or anyone else to be at the center of it. But it took me a lifetime to figure this out." Pete's voice trailed off, his eyes reflecting the shame and regret of the decades he felt he lost.

"More and more, as time goes by, we learn to live a life of self-sacrifice. Some learn it quicker than others, like my friend Dave. But, well, I suppose not everyone learns this lesson."

"If you were my grandpa, Pete, I'd definitely miss you if you died. But when it comes to my gramps, or even my dad, well…".

Suddenly Pete crawled from the shelter as quickly as he could, his head spinning. When he was certain Travis couldn't see him he quietly burst into tears. Images of his children when they were young, and of his grandchildren, flooded his mind. It was that he might never again experience the sweet innocence and unguarded love of the young, that pained him, and that maybe Travis had never known this. Pete grieved for the loss of all of it.

"Pete, are you okay?", Travis shouted from the shelter. "Did I say something wrong?"

Pete struggled to compose himself. "No, no, Travis, I'm okay. But thanks. I—I just felt some nausea coming on. I think I'm okay now. Be back inside in a second."

Then he pulled his empty flask from his jacket pocket, along with a picture of his grandchildren, taken the previous Christmas. He glanced back forth between both objects. Though inches apart, each represented parts of his life that felt infinitely separated.

Dave never got to taste this, Lord, he thought. *To be delighted in by loved ones. He lived a hard life with a hard dad and died a hard death. And…what about Travis? Will he end up the same way? I fear he will, and this fills me with grief. I couldn't save Dave, and maybe I can't save Travis, either. So what good am I? What good is it to be brokenhearted for those you can't really help?*

"I only call on you to love and to trust. Nothing more," came the words so clearly that he thought he was hallucinating from his fever.

Pete crawled back inside the shelter. As he was putting his flask back in his pack Travis caught sight of it. "There's no rum left in your flask, Pete. Remember? It all spilled out."

Pete nodded his head in affirmation, a faint, sad smile on his face. He was about to slide into his sleeping bag, but hesitated. Then he eased himself down on the packed snow of the shelter floor, and leaned back against the wall. His joints ached more than he'd realized, and he was dizzy and winded, all bad signs he tried to ignore. He closed eyes as he spoke, trying to stay focused.

"Travis…um, tell me more about yourself," he said between labored breaths.

"You don't sound good, Pete. Shouldn't you lie down?"

Pete smiled weakly. "I'm okay for now. What, uh, what do you study at CU?"

"Speech communication."

"Why that? What do you do with that kind of degree?"

"Good question, Pete," Travis snorted. "I wish I knew. I wanted to get into the journalism school, but my grades weren't good enough. So this was the next best thing I guess."

"Do you like it? I'm asking because your heart doesn't seem in it."

"I ask myself that all the time, Pete. But what's the alternative? Drop out? My dad would disown me."

Pete felt his stomach knot up, but not because he was ill. Travis's words were all too familiar, even all these decades later. Something inside him wanted to punch Travis's dad in the nose. *The damn injus-*

tice of it all! The conditional love and rejection. I hate it, Lord. I really do. Where's the love? Then Pete cooled down.

"What makes your heart come alive, Travis?"

"Huh?"

"What are you passionate about? What do you get excited about?"

"Girls".

"Of course you do, but besides that?"

"I guess I'd say rock-and-roll. When I was a kid my mom would drop me off at my grandma's house every so often, so she could go do errands or whatever. This one time I was exploring the basement of my grandma's house, and I found an old record player. And there were some old albums nearby. The one that grabbed my attention was 'A Hard Day's Night', by the Beatles. The music and the images of the Beatles captivated me, ya know? I listened to it over and over, scratching the hell out of it because I couldn't hold that damn needle still!"

Travis let out a hearty laugh. Suddenly Pete realized it was the first time he'd ever seen the lighter side of him.

"After that I became obsessed with the Beatles, but also rock music in general. We had an old acoustic guitar. I'm not even sure where we got it. But eventually I convinced my parents to buy me a used electric guitar and an amp. It was kind of beat up, but it was a Fender Stratocaster, which is a well-made guitar. It was black and white, like the kind Jimi Hendrix would sometimes play. Do you know who Jimi Hendrix is, Pete?"

Pete shook his head no. "Sorry, son. I was always too old for the music of that generation."

"That's okay. I understand. Anyway, I practiced all the time. Truthfully, too much, because I'd avoid my homework to practice. This made my parents so mad. But one day I left my guitar out, on the floor. I'm not sure why. My dad asked me to put it away, but I forgot. The next morning, he got up early to go to work, and tripped over the guitar. He hit the floor and jacked up his hand. He was so mad that he grabbed the guitar, went into the garage, and smashed it into the concrete floor. I cried when I found out. But he didn't even apologize. He just said that me losing the guitar was a 'natural consequence' of a bad choice. I guess I never really got over that one. I mean, he did a lot of bad shit, but that one really hurt."

Pete couldn't turn his eyes from Travis. The hurt seemed to ooze out of him like poison. All Pete could offer was, "I'm sorry, son. Your dad was wrong. You didn't deserve that." He wanted to say more, but was simply too exhausted now. Then he wiggled into his sleeping bag.

8 - THE QUEEN CITY OF THE PLAINS

The Santa Fe sped west, its whistle echoing from one horizon to the other as the train gobbled up miles of track and parted the prairie grass. Pete lay awkwardly in a booth in the dining car, eyes closed and feeling as though every muscle in his body had cramped up. The train's whistle blew, long and loud in the dry October air. Pete smiled.

The Chief rolled into Denver's Union Station the next day. The Rocky Mountains lay before Pete. He was speechless. They were unlike anything he'd ever seen. The highest peaks were barren and pure white, blanched from an early, high-country storm. It almost hurt the eyes to look at them, shimmering against the deep blue. Longs Peak, to the north, held his gaze. Its long, sweeping east ridge and square top dominated the Front Range, distant, monolithic, and foreboding. Many passengers paused a moment to look at the range, then went about their business disembarking.

Pete hopped off the train and passed beneath Union Station's arch. He strolled south and east on Sixteenth Street, which lay before him like a tree heavy with low-hanging fruit.

I'd like to work on a ranch. But how do I find a job like that? I should head toward the stock yards. Aren't there stock yards in Denver? There has to be, but which way? I'll go find a decent store or a service station and ask someone.

The air wasn't too crisp, warming rapidly in the sun since early morning. It would be a warm day, but random gusts reminded Pete that winter was on its way. The street crowds were thick, at least for Pete, everyone with somewhere to go or something to do, or so it seemed. Taxis—how long had it been since he'd seen one?—came and went. A trolley rang its bell and pulled up as clusters of people got off and on while they clutched brown grocery bags, purses and briefcases, even a hat box. A young man in an alley, wearing a coverall, carried a small crate on his shoulder from the back of a truck across a loading dock. He disappeared through a heavy, dark green, dented steel door that was propped open. A man in a shirt and tie swept the area around the front entrance of a department store on the first floor of a large, four-story building with the word STEEL's affixed high up on its facade. Nearby, two men appeared to be in an intense discussion while a rumpled old man sold apples for five cents each on the corner of Sixteenth Street and Welton Avenue.

Pete turned down Welton and headed north and east. When he passed the main business district on Seventeenth Street, he made a mental note to go back there to begin his job search. His eye caught a large sign in the distance on the roof of a small building that said HOTEL WYNNE. He walked over to the hotel, which was next to a small, busy auto repair garage, and booked a room for one night only. He grabbed the key from the clerk and took the stairs up to his room, 407.

The small, austere room was hot and stuffy and smelled like the inside of his grandparents' house. He opened the window to cool the room down and lay on the bed to see how soft it was. The last time he laid on a regular bed was back in his parents' house.

Anxious, he wandered back to Welton for more exploration. At Twentieth Street he turned west, toward the mountains.

"Yes," he said, as the Front Range stretched out before him again, "this is more like it."

He went a half-dozen blocks before catching the whiff of locomotive smoke and heard the rhythmic ding of a switcher's bell: Denver's train yard. His eyes narrowed. He stroked the thin growth on his chin.

"Maybe I'll just wander over and see if anyone needs an extra man."

At the train yard locomotives sat idling everywhere. Wisps of smoke from sizzling boilers disappeared into the sunny sky while little switchers darted about, shunting freight and passenger cars among the iron giants with a jolt here and a bang there. There were men all over, some shouting, most just doing their jobs. Pete didn't see any cattle cars yet, but he knew they must be somewhere, hidden from view. A long freight train lumbered slowly through the yard, heading somewhere south. Pete kept his wits about him as he hopped over the numerous rails on his way to the yard manager's office.

The office of the manager was dark compared to the outside. Pete waited for his eyes to adjust. An older, heavyset, bosomy secretary in a cotton dress banged away on a typewriter. She looked up at Pete momentarily, resumed typing, and said with a Western lilt, "The Rio Grande already sent your order papers over. You can just grab 'em and head out."

Pete wasn't sure what to say for a moment, then, fumbling, spat out, "Uh, I'm here for a possible job."

"Oh, are you one of the guys left over from the Denver, South Park, and Pacific? It's a shame the D&RGW put you all out of business. Such a tough little railroad too. Leadville will miss you. Anyway, the Rio Grande ain't sent nothin' over yet for you DSP&P boys, so we really don't know who you are or where you're supposed to be. You'll just have to wait some more. Sorry, I know times is tough."

"Uh, well, I'm not with anyone, ma'am. I don't know if you can use an extra hand, or you know anyone who can, but I thought I'd ask."

In a tone somewhere between annoyance and pity, she said, "Oh, well, I can't help you about that. You'll have to talk to Mr. Larsen, though I don't recall him needing anyone right now."

"Is he available?"

"He should be back shortly; he's up on the far end of the yard. Somebody had a real mess loading some cattle. He'll probably be a bit vexed, I should warn you. He always gets that way when he has to deal with livestock. He's sort of fussy about his clothes and keeping clean and all." The secretary giggled, then added, "Kind of ironic given that he runs a train yard. But he gets by."

Pete thanked her and sat down on a smooth wooden bench near the door, in a spot where the varnish and stain had worn through. He bit his thumbnail and examined it like a diamond cutter. The clicking bursts of the typewriter and the steady ticks of the clock filled the room in a jazz-like riff, even against the clatter of locomotives and rolling stock out in the yard.

Finally, the door burst open and a small, impish man hustled in. He wore round glasses and his hair was combed all the way over to cover his balding head. He smelled like manure, his heavy khaki trousers dark brown near the cuffs. He wore cowboy boots and cussed as he tried scraping them off on the mat near the door. His shirt sleeves were rolled up, and his bolo tie was tight against his throat.

"Damn it, Agnes," Larsen whined. "The next time somebody wants to desecrate my yard with too much livestock, you tell them to go to hell! Or at least send Jack or Tony to clean it up. I don't need this! Why the hell am I the only one capable of keeping this yard in order?" he asked as he slammed shut the door to his office, rattling the privacy glass.

Agnes rolled her eyes and flashed a disconcerting smile Pete's way as she got up and popped her head in Larsen's office. Muffled, exasperated tones spilled through the crack in the doorway. Back and forth the conversation went on, like a scrum in a rugby game. Then Agnes drew her head back out and shut the door abruptly.

"Mr. Larsen will see you in a few moments, young man. What is your name?"

"Peter McGregor."

"Well, it's very nice to meet you, Peter. I'm Agnes."

"Ma'am," was all Pete said as he tilted his head toward her.

Minutes passed again, and Agnes banged away on her typewriter. Pete's mouth went dry as Larsen emerged. He walked up to Pete, who stood. Larsen didn't offer his hand. He spoke quickly.

"What is your name?"

"Peter McGregor, sir."

"Have you worked on a railroad before, Peter?"

"No sir."

"When did you come out here?"

"I just got in today."

Larsen's eyes widened and his brow arched. "Oh my, that was quick." He laughed in a nervous, high-pitched way. "Well, Peter, I'm sorry I can't help you. We have all the men we need. Jobs are hard to come by nowadays, as I'm sure you know. The Depression is hard on everyone. Best of luck to you."

Larsen then gave a curt, stiff wave of his hand, turned, and scurried back to his office, shutting the door quietly.

"Thank you for your time, ma'am," Pete said to Agnes.

Bent over her typewriter, trying to adjust or fix something, Agnes didn't look up. "Oh, okay. You're welcome, Paul. You have a good day now."

Pete frowned, shook his head, and left slowly, out the door and across the yard. He paused a few times, watching the switchers, and thought about hopping on an empty cattle train heading north, probably into Wyoming. He wandered back toward downtown instead.

Low in the sky, just before it disappeared behind the Front Range, the sun turned orange and gilded the clouds above it. Pete had never seen a sunset quite like it.

The Hotel Wynne wasn't far from the train yard, but Pete was too edgy to sit in his room. The air had a bite to it now, and Pete unrolled the sleeves on his battered flannel shirt. In the theater district on Sixteenth Street a restaurant with a gaudy neon sign that said CHOP SUEY caught his attention. He walked in, the only customer in the small, clean restaurant at this time of day. A small Chinese man greeted him with a menu. He wore a traditional Chinese smock, blue with white buttons all the way up, and wide, black trousers.

In a thick accent he said, "You only customer right now, have pick of table."

There were five tables to choose from. Pete picked one of the small ones, next to the large, plate glass window. The man who'd greeted him brought a small, white, porcelain pot of steaming tea and a cup and saucer. Pete's family used to go out for Chinese food, on Cleveland's east side, for many years. He poured the tea, then added so much sugar that it caught the Chinese man's attention. Pete held the little tea cup with both hands and let the steam from it waft over his face.

Outside the window, across the street, next to a theater lit up with more bulbs than Pete had ever seen, two ragged men sat on the sidewalk, sharing half of a dark loaf of bread. Their thick, sluggish movements looked frail to Pete as they broke the bread apart and chewed it for what seemed like forever. When they were finished, one of them pulled out a pint of whiskey. It slipped from his fingers and shattered on the pavement, staining it temporarily dark as the liquid spread toward the street. The one who dropped it sprang into action and dabbed his fingers in the spilled alcohol repeatedly, touching them to his mouth each time. He licked his lips, sat back down again, and pressed his back into the wall of the theater building.

The sky was bright orange now, the clouds reflecting the day's departing glory as the business district went from half-light to darker shades with shadows strewn here and there. The two men across the street stood and sort of huddled together as they looked at the sidewalk, still wet from the broken bottle of whiskey. One said something to the other, pulled out a wallet, and extracted a small picture. He smiled, his teeth gleaming against his dark, stubbly face, as he showed the little picture to the other man. Nonplussed, the other man shuffled on, urging his friend to accompany him with a tilt of his head. Pete watched the men disappear from view, like human schooners laboring over a sea of concrete, their sagging shoulders heavy beneath their dull, gray trench coats.

The Chinese man arrived at his table, and Pete ordered two entrees: chop suey and egg foo young. They arrived, steaming hot, a short time later. He devoured the greasy food, then asked for his check. An argument in Chinese spilled into the dining room from somewhere in the kitchen. Instead of the man, a Chinese woman emerged with Pete's bill. He laid down a few bills and didn't bother to wait for change.

When he stood up to leave, his stomach began doing cartwheels. His throat tightened. Knowing he'd vomit at any moment and preferring to do so out in the street, he shoved a few chairs aside as he bolted for the front door. But he tripped instead and toppled a table. Plates, silverware, and glasses crashed to the floor as his stomach heaved its chunky, pinkish liquid. The woman screamed.

Pete staggered to his feet, ready to leave as best he could in order to retain any shred of dignity. The Chinese man rushed up, grabbed his sleeve, and said, "You no leave! You stay and pay for mess! You no leave or I call police. You pay for mess."

Pete wiped his mouth with his sleeve. "I'm very sorry, sir. Please forgive me. I can't pay you. I don't have any money left."

"You have no money? How you pay bill then? You lie! You have money."

"No, I'm honestly out of money. I just paid you the last of what I have. I don't have any money left."

The Chinese man let go of Pete, thought for a moment, then responded, "You stay, wash dishes, pay for mess. You work for free."

Pete ran for the front door. He stumbled out onto the sidewalk and back the way he'd come.

The man ran after him, shouting, "Police! Help, police! Thief! Thief! You stop! You come back, pay for mess!"

The early evening crowd, headed for a play or a movie, gawked at the spectacle. Some laughed while others pointed and whispered to their companions. Nobody made a move. Pete kept running as the Chinese man's voice faded behind him. Suddenly a cop dashed out of an alley and collided with Pete. Both men tumbled to the pavement. The cop got up first and stood over Pete as the Chinese man came running up. The ground and sky spun as Pete lay there, listening to the man explain everything to the cop. Pete rose up and held onto the cop to steady himself.

"Is what he said true, mac?" the officer asked Pete, pushing his cap back and scratching his forehead.

Pete wiped his mouth again. "Yes, officer, but it was an accident, honest. I had to throw up, so I tried to get out of there as fast as I could, but I tripped."

"Well, I understand that, son, but someone still has to pay for the mess, and since you caused it, you gotta cough up the dough. I'm sorry, but that's just the way life works sometimes."

"But I don't have any money left," Pete protested. "I paid the bill with the last of my money."

The officer frowned and let out a sigh. He pulled his cap back down, low over his forehead. Seconds passed. Then he cocked his head and looked sideways at Pete.

"Then I guess you're going to have to work for free until you pay for the mess you made."

"Okay. But how will I eat if I don't get paid?"

"I'm sure Mr. Chu will be happy to give you your meals for free until you've worked off your debt, right, Mr. Chu?" the cop said, nodding toward the Chinese man.

"Yes, that fine," Mr. Chu said.

"Does he know of a place I can stay for free?"

"Mr. Chu, do you have any extra rooms for rent?" Then, turning to Pete, the cop added, "He rents a few rooms out of his house."

"Yes, I have room, in basement, though. You stay for free till you work off what you owe. That seem fair to me."

"That seems fair to me, too, Mr. Chu." The cop turned to Pete again. "Sounds like a decent offer to me, son. I'd take it unless you want to spend some time in the hoosegow. What do ya think?"

Pete bowed his head and nodded.

He worked off his debt in a few weeks, then figured he'd stay on for the meager wage Mr. Chu paid him until he could find something better. He washed dishes, mopped floors, and took out the trash. Chu even taught him how to cook a bit. The kitchen was hot and humid, even on the coldest days. Mr. Chu gave Pete a fresh, crisp, white uniform to wear on the days he worked.

At the end of his shift the ritual was always the same. Pete tossed his soiled shirt in a laundry hamper, put on his street clothes, and said, "I'm done with my work, Mr. Chu."

"Okay, Peter. When you come back to work?"

"Tomorrow, Mr. Chu," he'd say, or maybe "Not till Tuesday, Mr.

Chu," and he'd exit through the back door into the shadows of the alley and the dry, cool air laced with whiffs of rotting cabbage, noodles, and garlic.

He didn't eat breakfast in order to save money. He ate lunch and dinner for a nominal fee at Mr. Chu's restaurant. He saved enough, too, for a few extra items of clothing. In the late mornings and the days he had off, he'd wander the streets of Denver, exploring, thinking, plotting his next move. He also made sure he was never without a pint of whiskey.

He walked the streets after work, too, avoiding sleep as much as he could. He hadn't slept straight through the night almost since he'd arrived in Denver.

In the beginning of February 1936, Pete discovered a little mountaineering and ski shop—Lon's Alpin Haus it was called—wedged in between a men's haberdashery and a fix-it shop on Glenarm Street. The inside smelled like new wool and fresh, polished leather. Sweaters, gabardine slacks and coats, shiny leather ski boots, and wooden skis from the Groswold Ski Company filled the shelves and almost every inch of space in the store. There were even ice axes, ring pitons, climbing ropes, and hobnailed boots from Italy. The owner, Lon, had a full, reddish-brown beard and smoked a pipe that scented the cramped store with the sweet odor of pipe tobacco. His voice was deep and calm, and Pete liked the sound of it.

Pete frequented Lon's store increasingly as spring approached, though he couldn't afford anything. Lon didn't seem to mind. Pete liked the hardware the most, running his hands over the smooth, polished wood of the skis and ice axes, the rough hemp of the climbing ropes, and the hard points on the bottom of the hobnailed boots. Images burst in his mind, like splotches of bright paint, of crisp, white snow, deep-blue skies, and gray, craggy rocks. Worlds he'd never known, wild, pure, and dangerous.

He and Lon talked about many things: right and wrong, riches and poverty, God, skiing, mountain climbing, adventure. Pete especially loved to hear about Lon's adventures in Colorado and Europe.

In mid-April, on a cold, overcast day when Pete wasn't scheduled to work, he spent most of the morning talking to Lon and helping him, as Lon switched his inventory from skiing to mountaineering equipment in anticipation of summer. A picture hanging on the wall caught his attention.

"Where was this picture taken, Lon?"

"In Navajo Basin, just west of Telluride."

"What peaks are those tall ones?"

"Mount Wilson and El Diente. Each one is over fourteen thousand feet."

Everything about the picture looked wild and beautiful to Pete. Something inside him seemed to ache to be in the picture, to be in that remote place.

"I've never heard you talk about it. How come?"

"Well, maybe I'll tell you later. Let's get the inventory finished. Could you move the rest of the skis and poles to the storage room, please?"

"Sure," Pete said, and did as Lon requested. It took him until lunch, and he ruminated the whole time about whether he should ask Lon more questions.

"Let's go over to the Buckhorn for some lunch, Pete. My treat."

At the Buckhorn Pete nursed a bottle of Coca-Cola as Lon talked about a theological issue, but Pete only listened halfheartedly. He still wanted to know about Lon's trip to Mount Wilson and El Diente. He figured something bad must have happened but, being young and relatively unscathed by life, couldn't understand why Lon wouldn't talk about a place so wild and captivating.

"Lon, what happened in Navajo Basin?"

"It didn't go too well."

"How so?"

The waitress brought their meals, and Lon carefully spread his napkin on his lap and added some sugar to his refreshed cup of coffee. He grabbed his knife and fork and was about to cut into a pork chop. Then he stopped and looked up.

"I lost a friend on El Diente, Pete. And it was my fault."

Oh, I see. I wasn't trying to be nosy. I'll let it go."

"He was my climbing partner, had been for years. We fought together in the Great War. We climbed a lot of mountains, the two of us: the Diamond Face on Longs Peak, with Carl Blaurock and Bill Irvin. We were even with them when Blaurock did his famous headstand on Sunlight Peak in the Needles Range. It was special, Pete.

"It was late July, but the spring of '26 was cold and wet, so there was still a lot of snow up high, even though it was well into summer. We were in a little snow gully near the top of El Diente. We had to use our ice axes. My friend was down below me, about twenty yards. I had to chop a step into a section of rock that was coated with ice. I made the little notch in the ice and stepped across to a muddy patch. My boot sank into the mud. A boulder about the size of a basketball broke loose. I screamed 'Rock!' and looked down."

Lon grabbed his napkin quickly and dabbed his eyes.

"The...uh...rock glanced off his head. He went down in a heap. I almost tumbled off the mountain scrambling down to him. It was horrible."

Lon covered his eyes with one hand and rubbed his face. Pete felt stupid and didn't know what to do or say.

Eyes closed, Lon forced his words out.

"There was blood everywhere, Peter. And I knew there was just no way . . ."

Lon looked away for a minute and tried to swallow the lump in his throat.

"It was a heck of a job getting his body out. It probably took me three times longer than a normal hike out."

Pete slumped lower in his chair as he traced a circular pattern in his gravy with his knife. He ate slowly and quietly.

Lon hadn't touched his lunch. He pulled out his pipe and took his time stuffing and packing it with tobacco. He lit it, and a cloud of new smoke enveloped his face.

"Scars, Peter. We all carry scars and ghosts in our lives. You do your best to make peace with them. In the end, you have to go on. But that's what adventure is like—there's no neutral ground. My partner, John, and I knew the risks. We calculated them and made our choices. The wound hurt more back then, but I have had to live with a scar that never seems to fade the older I get."

"Do you miss John?"

"I miss him every day."

Consequences, Pete thought. *Lon made an honest mistake, so now he has to pay for it for the rest of his life? Why, God? Aren't You supposed to be about love and mercy? If not, then I'm done for. I've made some really bad choices and hurt people. My parents have made many bad choices. Everyone makes bad choices. So are we all doomed? I certainly am, unless I can be perfect. Who the hell can be perfect?*

"Looking back, Lon, would you have done anything differently?"

"Of course, Peter. I would have chosen a different route up the mountain or made sure John was shielded from debris. But on a deeper level, would I have chosen not to climb mountains? Of course not."

"Why not?"

Lon set his knife and fork down and nestled his pipe in an ashtray, his forehead creased.

"We were meant for adventure, Peter. We were meant for life to the full. But to live that way means that you must accept the wounds that come with it. I wish it wasn't so. But what other choice is there? Live life avoiding all risk? Sure, you might avoid getting wounded, but you'll die having never really lived. We all die, right? But we all don't really live."

They finished lunch in near silence. Pete was stuck inside his head, trying to sort out what he believed. He craved adventure, but he also wanted to avoid the risks as much as he could. He felt stuck between both desires.

Lon paid the bill, and they walked back toward the store.

"Do you believe in God, Peter?"

"I'm not sure. Sometimes I feel like I'm supposed to. But I get scared, because I don't think I'm a very good person. So I think I avoid the subject, because who wants to think about burning in hell or whatever happens to bad people?"

"Indeed, Peter, that makes sense. But what if God wants you to think about Him, to believe in Him?"

"Am I supposed to spend my life in fear of hell then?"

Lon let out a knowing laugh with a grin and a quick wink of the eye. "Well, not quite. Let's just say there's a lot more to God than many people have been led to believe. It's not really about behaving yourself. It's about transformation, but we can discuss the rest some other time."

Pete gave Lon a puzzled look. Suddenly overcome with shame, he said, "I wasn't totally honest with you, Lon."

"How so?"

"Another reason I don't like thinking about God is because I'm afraid He's just like my dad. And, well, usually it seems that my dad is merely tolerating me, at best. I can't live up to his expectations. So how can I possibly live up to God's expectations?"

Lon laid a gentle hand on Pete's shoulder. "What if God isn't like your dad at all?"

Pete felt a kind of weight lift from his shoulders. Surprised, tears formed in his eyes. For the first time in his life Pete felt okay with who he was, and even let a ray of hope illuminate the darkness within, with the notion that perhaps he wasn't as despicable as he'd feared.

"When it gets warmer and the snow melts, let's go climbing," Lon said.

"I'd really like that, but I don't know how."

"I'll teach you, Peter."

"Really?" Fresh tears.

"When it gets warmer." Lon smiled and nodded.

In late May Lon took Pete up on the rocks in the foothills, where the snow had finally melted from the cracks and shadows. His favorite spot was on the short, tough pitches of rock that line the cliffs on the north side of the town of Golden. Though he was only of average height and his limbs weren't long, Pete excelled at climbing. His strength and athleticism made up for most of his inherent deficits. He seemed to have no fear either.

By mid-July Pete's skill had grown tremendously, and he began to surpass Lon on routes requiring more physical ability and less technical skill. It was now that Lon mentioned to Pete that he knew of a climbing outfit in the Grand Tetons. They were looking for a late-summer guide. He thought Pete was ready and, if Pete agreed, would contact them and recommend Pete. Pete readily accepted the offer.

Pete got the job. He didn't really have much money, so when it was time to leave, he rode the rails and hitched rides north and west, to the Tetons. He and Lon corresponded all summer, and Lon even sent him a few gifts: climbing pants, pitons and a hammer, and some extra hobnails for his boots.

Pete wrote of helping on guided expeditions, mostly comprised of rich Easterners, some who knew what they were doing and most who didn't. He bruised, scraped, and jammed his body into the tough, gray, craggy rocks of the Tetons. The pay wasn't great, but Pete had few expenses and was usually tipped for his hard work, at the end of an expedition. He was lean, tan, and hard bodied. He lived on beans and jerky, bacon and eggs, biscuits, fruit, and coffee. His life was simple but peaceful—"close to the bone," as he heard another guide say. It was the adventure he'd always craved. But the simple life eventually grew stale. He needed more—more adventure.

Pete returned to Denver in late September, a decent amount of cash in his pocket.

Lon offered him a job in his shop on the spot. He'd have to teach Pete how to ski since his inventory would be changing again, from mountaineering back to skiing, and Pete needed to be knowledgeable.

Lon was an expert skier. He'd gone to Dartmouth and was a member of the ski team. They were the best in the nation. He took Pete into the mountains in October, to St. Mary's Glacier, the only area close enough with any snow. He coached Pete through the rudiments of skiing, and as with mountain climbing, Pete learned and advanced quickly. Lon skied using the Arlberg Method, swinging his upper body to help initiate and execute turns more easily. His skis, and Pete's, were the latest technology had to offer—long wooden skis with metal edges.

In November Lon took Pete higher in the mountains, on steeper pitches in places above the timberline. They went up high, their skis on their shoulders and rucksacks on their backs, to places where the cold, gray, and pink rocks make you feel like you're trespassing on something sacred and foreign.

By Christmas time Lon let Pete begin selling ski equipment. He even used him on occasion as a guinea pig to test some of the latest gear. And like his time in the Tetons, Pete relished the new challenges, the daily and weekly little adventures that framed his days.

One day, a few weeks before Christmas, Lon and Pete were putting up a Christmas tree in the store. They chatted while they worked.

"Will you need time off for the holidays, Peter?"

"Not really, Lon, maybe just a few days. I thought maybe we could get up into the high country and do some more skiing."

"Well, I can't really leave the shop. It's the busiest time of the year."

"Do you not want me to take time off?"

"No, no. I'll be okay without you for a few days. How will you get into the mountains?"

"I'm not really sure. I thought maybe I'd be able to hop on the Rio Grande. I'm pretty good at it."

"How will you manage with all your equipment?"

"I was thinking I'd put my boots in my rucksack and tie my skis and poles together. That way I'd really only have a couple of bundles to worry about."

"Tell you what, Peter. Why don't you just take my car?"

"Are you sure?"

"I am."

"Thank you, Lon." He wasn't going to say more, then suddenly added, "It seems like God has been looking out for me a lot since I left home. I don't know why I haven't noticed until now."

"It's a strange phenomenon with human beings—we only seem to really learn from pain. Success doesn't seem to teach us much."

"I guess I'm just beginning to understand what you mean, Lon."

They finished setting up the Christmas tree, then added the ornaments and tinsel. Before moving on to other tasks, Lon paused.

"I meant to ask you something, Peter. How come you're not going home for the holidays? You're from the east, right? Cincinnati?"

"Cleveland, actually."

"Ah yes, that's right. I remember now. So why aren't you hopping a train back home for Christmas?"

"Well, you can't afford to be without my help for that long, can you?"

"I could manage for something like that. Family is very important."

Pete nodded but said nothing.

"So why aren't you going home, Peter?"

Pete shrugged. "There's really nothing to go home to. As I've said before, my dad barely tolerates me. And I'm not close with my mom either."

Lon said nothing, looking as though he was trying to solve a puzzle.

"Why do you think it's like this with your parents?"

"I don't seem to be very good at relationships, Lon. I guess I learned this from my parents. I'm sure they learned it from their parents. So maybe it's not surprising I don't miss them."

Lon was about to speak. Instead he searched Pete's eyes but for what? Pete sensed Lon's curiosity somehow and continued.

"I know I should miss them, but there's really nothing to miss. My dad's life is the company, and my mom likes to drown her sorrows in the bottle. So where do I fit in?"

"But you are their son."

"That's what I used to tell myself," Pete said, looking away. He quickly wiped away a tear.

"But you don't anymore?"

"No."

"Why not?"

Pete shrugged. "I dunno."

"I think perhaps that you do know, Peter, but you'd rather avoid the subject, eh?"

"Hell, maybe I don't want to avoid it, Lon, but it hurts to admit that maybe they care more about themselves than they do about me or my brother and sister. After a while you give up because you lose heart. You get tired of carrying around the empty hope that maybe someday they'll be the parents you want."

"Peter, what if no one can live up to what any of us wants?"

"Then…then we're stuck. It means we all have a big problem that can't be solved. That seems to make life pointless somehow, as if life is only about pain."

Pete felt a firm hand on his shoulder. Lon turned him around until they faced each other fully.

"Peter," Lon said in a firm but weary voice, "sooner or later everyone gets disappointed. It's too much to ask another human being to meet a desire that only God can meet. And...the crazy thing is that if we let God meet our every need, then we're free to love others without demands. The pressure is off then. Does this make sense to you?"

"I don't know. But does God ever disappoint you as well?"

"Yes, to be honest. Sometimes He does."

"So then what?"

A knowing kind of look came over Lon. "Those are the times I have to remind myself that God probably knows what He's doing even if I don't."

Several months later, Pete reported for work one day sunburned from a warm day of late-season skiing the day before. He looked like a raccoon with white patches around his eyes from his glacier goggles. Lon had the door open. It was late morning and already balmy. The sweet scent from Lon's pipe wafted out the door and rolled down the sidewalk. Pete smelled it as soon as he turned onto Glenarm. He smiled and nodded knowingly to himself.

Lon had him organize and sweep one of the back storage rooms. Pete shuffled back and forth to and from the retail floor. On one of his little trips he overheard Lon talking to a man at the counter. They talked of climbing, and it seemed they had been on an adventure or two. Lon called Pete over.

"Peter, have you given any thought to college? You've told me you were educated in private schools. Were your parents going to send you to college?"

"Of course, Lon. There was never a question as to whether or not I would go. The only question was where?"

"But you didn't go because you ran away, right?"

Pete nodded as he avoided Lon's gaze.

"It's my assumption they have some kind of a trust fund set up for you for college and for the rest of your life. Am I correct?"

"Definitely. It's a sizable trust."

"Why haven't you accessed it? You're of age, aren't you?"

"Yes, but my dad added a clause to the trust stipulating that he gets to determine when I'll be given sole ownership of it. Right now, he's still the executor."

"Have you contacted him and asked that you be granted full ownership?"

"You don't know my dad, Lon. The fact that I left home and haven't contacted him in over a year has enraged him, I'm sure. He most likely has taken it as a personal affront. I upset his plans. Now he can't control me. And I'm sure I've embarrassed him."

"I see. Well, do you want to go to college?"

"Yes, Lon, someday."

"Peter, I've never really told you about my family. Have you wondered?"

"Yes, but I figured it's your business and if you wanted to tell me, you would."

Lon grabbed his pipe and began packing the bowl for a smoke. His hands shook, just a little. Pete never noticed this before.

"I had a wife and two sons, Peter," Lon said softly. "They were all killed in a car accident in the fall of 1924. My boys were very young, just toddlers. And my wife and I hadn't been married long.

"Years before, I'd inherited a nice little sum of money from a great-aunt of mine. I was her favorite. Anyway, I took the money and invested it for a long time. But I pulled it out of the stock market as the crash was just getting started. I managed to salvage a decent amount of it. It was supposed to be for my sons, for college."

It was silent in the shop. A passing car honked its horn, and a trolley rang its bell as it rumbled past. Pete began to speak, but no words came out.

"I miss my family, Peter," Lon mumbled. "My younger son, Nicholas, had this way of smiling at me that was . . ." Lon's voice died away, and he shook his head slowly. "Anyway, I'd like you to have the money, son."

Pete didn't know what to do. He held out his hand weakly. "Lon, I'm so sorry for what happened to you. Your offer is incredibly generous. I wish I knew what more to say."

"You don't have to, son. I know you'll put it to good use wherever you enroll."

"What were your sons' names?"

"James and Nicholas."

Pete's lips curled, and again he didn't know what to say. Then he summoned his courage to ask, "How did you go on after you lost your family and your best friend? I don't mean any disrespect, Lon, but I think I would've ended my life. That's too much pain. I don't understand how you've been able to go on."

"Neither do I sometimes. It often seems that dying is easy. It's living that's the hard part. But I've learned that God can create beauty from ashes. It takes a long time, but it happens, day by day, a moment at a time. There's a bigger story out there. I'm committed to that, and that gives me hope."

Pete nodded, wishing he understood more of what Lon said, but glad some of it made sense.

9 - HIGHER EDUCATION

"That's Old Main, in case you were wondering."

Pete was shielding his eyes from the bright August sun, staring up at the four-story building that was the heart and soul of the campus at the University of Colorado in Boulder. Pete was accepted for the fall term of 1938.

Though Germany, Italy, and Japan were dragging a reluctant world toward war, Pete had other concerns. He didn't know what he would study in college, beyond the basics. And he worried that perhaps his academic skills were dull now, as it had been over three years since he was in school.

He turned toward the person speaking to him, a young man like Pete, but professorial looking. He was taller and athletic looking. He wore round spectacles, and his hair was slicked back. He reminded Pete of a blond Aldous Huxley.

"Excuse me?"

"That building you're staring at, that's Old Main. It was the first building constructed. Are you new to CU?"

"Yeah. I guess that's where I'm supposed to check in."

"Well, sure, unless of course you weren't interested in going to college," the man said dryly.

Pete let out an amused snort. "What's your name?"

"Dave Bates, last time I checked." He thrust a large hand toward Pete. "And you are?"

"Pete McGregor," he said, returning the gesture. "You look like a professor, but I'm guessing you're an upperclassman."

"Wrong on both accounts," Dave said, punctuating this with an upraised index finger. Again Pete laughed. "I'm a graduate student. I'm working on my doctorate in civil engineering."

"Ah, one of those smart types."

"I've got 'em all fooled actually."

"Doubtful, but I wouldn't really know. I'm definitely not an engineer. I'm more of an English or history major type. It's too bad, too, because our paths probably won't cross again."

"Probably not, unless you like to ski."

Pete smiled.

By the middle of the following school year Pete and Dave were best friends. As was their custom, they were venturing into the high country for a day of skiing up on Berthoud Pass. It was almost spring now.

Dave had driven, running late as usual. Pete threw his gear into the trunk. It seemed as though Dave brought every piece of equipment for every possible contingency they might face, which always made Pete laugh to himself. *That's the professor, meticulous as always*, he thought. Pete grabbed his heavy leather ski boots last and placed them inside the car to keep them warm.

They drove west into the Rockies, easy on the gas and the brake, up, down, and around the various passes and hills. A storm had dumped several feet of dry, light snow, and the far winter sun shined clearly in the cobalt-blue sky, refracting off millions of crystals of snow like an endless sea of tiny diamonds. Stand after stand of blue spruce, Douglas fir, and lodgepole pine silently rolled by. Encrusted in thick coats of snow, the trees looked like they had been caked in powdered sugar.

It took Pete and Dave almost four hours to travel the sixty miles to the top of Berthoud Pass. Since the pass ran north and south, and access from Denver necessitated a southerly approach, long stretches of the dirt road were clear of snow in the winter sunshine. The road up Berthoud Pass was regularly plowed, had been for a few years, but sometimes, like this day, it was still impassable for motor cars.

Pete and Dave drove as high as they could until the snow became too deep. Dave parked the car a mile or so below the summit of the pass, which topped out at eleven thousand feet, not too far below the tree line. They donned their rucksacks, put on their ski boots, hoisted their skis atop their shoulders, and hiked up. They were dressed in wool slacks and turtlenecks, with their extra layers in their packs. It was sunny, so they wore glacier goggles. The air was so thin that they had to take short breaks every five to ten minutes, even though they were young and fit. By the time they reached the top, about an hour later, sweat flowed freely down their faces and backs.

They dropped their packs with a sigh and strapped on their long, wooden skis. Pete could afford the best equipment, a convenient by-product of working in a ski shop. Both men had long, bamboo poles with large baskets on the end. Their bindings were called bear traps; the heels of their ski boots moved freely but could be locked in place for going downhill. This was done by hooking a thick, flexible spring under a lip on the back of the boot, then tightening it by locking it down in the front part of the binding.

Standing at the top of Berthoud Pass, Pete went first, as always, plunging down the shaded north side. His turns were sloppy, wild, and aggressive. But he was fast. He stopped a good distance down the slope, turned, and watched Dave come down, whose Arlberg turns were smooth, controlled, and precise. In the trees, Dave caught up to Pete and coached him through them. They reached the bottom, almost a thousand feet down, took off their skis, placed them on their shoulders, and slogged back up. After a couple of runs, it was time for something to eat.

They sat up on the pass, facing south, toward the sun. They ate French bread with Brie cheese, fruit, and rich, European chocolate. Pete had brought a bottle of wine too. After their fete they lay down on the snow.

"Dave, do you think you've suffered in life?"

"Huh?"

"I know, it's a weird question."

"Everyone has, Pete. But all things considered, I have it pretty good. We both do."

"Sure, but why do you think God has allowed you to suffer? I don't know anyone closer to the Almighty than you."

"God's people have always suffered, Pete. Read a Bible and you'll see."

Pete sat up and turned to Dave, whose face was placid, waxen-looking as he basked in the spring sun.

"But that doesn't answer my question."

Dave said nothing at first. Pete looked at his own boots, the sun melting the snow on them, turning the leather wet and dark. His face felt hot in the late-winter sunshine. A sudden gust of wind snatched icy flakes off a nearby drift and scattered them about, hitting Pete in the face and cooling him off. Then the air was still.

"There are things God wants to teach us that can only be learned through suffering, unfortunately. It's just the way it is."

"Like what?"

Dave opened his eyes and sat up. He stared at the patch of snow between his knees, then traced patterns in it with his finger. He turned to Pete, head cocked.

"Like how to love and how to trust," Dave said softly, as though he was reminding himself.

"I never went to Sunday school, Dave, but that sounds like the kind of answer they teach you there."

Dave nodded, a distant look on his face. "Yeah, Pete, but you get older and you begin to learn what that really means."

A few hours later, as the sun marked its final path to the horizon, Pete and Dave made their last run, then scaled back to the top. Packs back on, they unlocked their bindings and kick-glided back down the pass. They were back at the car by the time the sun had dipped behind the highest western peaks. Neither talked much at first on the drive back down. Dave mentioned that he felt especially tired and asked Pete to drive. On the way back, Dave gazed out the car window as the purple dusk gathered in the valleys and shadows before engulfing everything in its dark, indigo blanket. They finished off the wine and the remainder of the food as they drove back to Boulder.

Pete got out when they reached his house, and Dave got back in the driver's seat.

"I had a great time, Dave."

Dave glanced at Pete a moment, then seemed distracted by the buttons on Pete's coat. "A lot of people had it good in the Roaring Twenties, Pete. But…I didn't. I lost my mom, and my dad did what he could to get us through it."

Pete was about to respond when Dave looked him in the eye and continued.

"It was a hard time, really hard."

Pete was ashamed to say anything, knowing how good the Twenties were to him and his family financially. Then his attention was diverted by two coeds hustling across the snow-packed street as they held their coats tight around their bodies. He turned back to Dave.

"If God gave you the power to change all that, would you, Dave?"

"I've asked myself the same question a lot. I used to think I would. But now I'm not so sure."

Something inside Pete told him not to reply, that what Dave had just said was somehow sacred and responding to it would desecrate it. He stared at his friend, who seemed mesmerized now by the steering wheel of his car. Then, almost before Pete realized it, Dave was off with a quick wave.

10 - SKIING MOUNTAIN MEN

It was the summer of 1943 now. Pete and Dave knew they'd be drafted, but they wanted to have some kind of say-so in the matter. So instead of waiting to be drafted, they enlisted in the Tenth Mountain Division, a new, elite unit of the army designed to train men to fight in the mountains and the cold. For the only time in its history, the army used civilians—experienced skiers—to recruit men with a background in skiing, mountaineering, trapping, and even mule skinning.

Captivated with the notion of the adventure that fighting in World War II promised, along with a desire to fight back against the tyranny of Germany and Japan, Pete had no problem deciding to enlist. Dave, on the other hand, being a bit older and having recently gotten married, needed more convincing. But soon he, too, was persuaded.

Pete moved his medium-sized, athletic frame out from under the clear, blue, endless July sky and relentless sun, and into the dark entryway of a troop train. A hot, dry wind blew dust and bits of paper around the platform of the Denver & Rio Grande Western Railroad. There were other young volunteers dressed in fresh uniforms, loitering in the stifling passageway between the train's regular passenger cars and the two set aside for military personnel. Pete was trying to figure out which of the identical cars might be the most comfortable.

On the platform Dave was in a heated discussion with his new wife, Lucy. Pete watched the argument for a moment, looked down when Dave glanced in his direction, then ducked inside the second troop car without looking back.

Inside he lumbered along with his heavy army duffel bag. The railcar was too narrow for him to hoist the bag over his shoulder, so he pushed and dragged the burden down the aisle, looking for two empty seats for himself and Dave. He found an empty seat at the far end of the darkened railcar. He dropped his duffel bag in the middle of the aisle and sat down with a thud.

Despite his estrangement from his family, Pete thought of them back in Cleveland. His older brother and his brother-in-law were probably in the midst of their workday by now, where they were probably very busy still learning how to take over and run the company from Robert McGregor, Pete's father: mountains of paperwork on mahogany desks, telephones ringing, stocks to watch, shipping schedules to maintain, personnel to manage. Like everyone, Pete's family kept track of the war. They followed the war's course in order to meet the supply demands of the United States' military and make sure the company's generous profits continued.

Pete gulped the last of his Coke as Dave walked up to his seat, likewise dragging his duffel bag. He rolled his eyes when he saw Pete, shook his head, and threw his bag onto the floor, next to Pete's.

"Nuts!" Dave said. "I never thought I'd find you. I'm tired of dragging this duffel up and down this godforsaken train. It has to be twenty degrees warmer here than outside. It feels like a gosh darn river of sweat is running down my back!"

"Geez, Dave, what's eating you?"

Dave wiped his brow with his sleeve, removed his serviceman's cap, and threw his tall, angular body onto the bench opposite Pete. He tilted back his head and closed his eyes. His blond hair was wet with sweat, like his forehead and upper lip.

"Ah, I'm sorry for whining, Pete. My darn wife is giving me the business for joining the mountain troops. She thinks a doctor of engineering belongs on campus. And with all due respect, it's different for you. You got your undergraduate degree in history."

"But she's had months to get used to it, right?"

"Well, she never thought I'd actually go! She figured I was caught up in the moment, that's all."

Dave got up, took off his coat, loosened his tie, and laid his tall frame down along the full length of the bench. Then he shut his eyes and draped his arm over his face.

"Well, she figured wrong, is all I can say," Pete replied.

The train's whistle echoed high and long off the surrounding, gray buildings. Their car jerked, lurched forward, then eased away from the platform. Pete glanced out the window. Lucy was walking away, her light-colored summer dress blowing sideways in the hot wind. She placed her hand on her wide-brimmed hat to keep it from blowing away. She didn't look back.

The troop train strained and clanged its way south from Denver, toward Pueblo, before heading west into the foothills of the Rockies, bound for the Arkansas River valley, Leadville, and eventually Camp Hale beyond.

The troop train exited a tunnel on a curve and a bolt of sunshine struck Pete in the face. The train snaked in and out of the shadows cast by the lower, rolling hills of the Rocky Mountains. The air was ten to fifteen degrees cooler now as they followed the Arkansas River toward the town of Salida. Leadville, Tennessee Pass, and Camp Hale itself lay beyond.

"What were you thinking about?" Dave said, who was awake and sitting upright. "I was thinking about all the times we've skied on Berthoud Pass."

"I miss those simpler times, Dave."

"Me too, Pete. But I'm guessing Hitler won't be apologizing anytime soon for complicating our lives."

"Well, that's 'Der Fuehrer,' always thinking only about himself!"

Four hours later the Denver and Rio Grande Western passenger and troop train eased its way into Leadville, as though it was grateful for the rest. It was early afternoon, and the afternoon thunderheads hadn't gathered enough force yet to blot out the sun or soak the earth, in booming ricochets of thunder. But the air was cool enough.

Leadville lay nestled in the mountains like an aging pageant queen, a memory of her former glory. There were still mining operations—specifically molybdenum mines up on Fremont Pass—but in Leadville it was only copper now.

Pete got up, stretched, and yawned loudly. "Okay, Dave, I'm going to go wet my whistle over at the Silver Dollar Bar. Want to join me?"

"Pete, what are you talking about? We've only got thirty minutes."

"Good, because that's five more minutes than I'll need."

"Pete, don't you dare miss this train."

"Well, if you come with me, you can make sure I get back on time."

"Come on, Pete, let's just go over to Davis Drug for a Coke instead."

"No way, Dave. Who knows how long it'll be before Uncle Sam lets us imbibe? I could go for some scotch, or bourbon, I think. No, wait, a gin and tonic would be perfect. Yes. It's the afternoon, right? My dad loves having a gin and tonic every afternoon. He calls them 'toddies' even though they aren't. I'll have a few and toast the SOB."

"Don't get carried away, Pete. You don't want to be listed AWOL before you even arrive at camp."

"Are you coming or not?"

"Fine. I'll go to make sure you get back on time. But a Coke is just fine with me."

A score of soldiers, and about half as many civilians, exited the train and headed for Leadville's business district, if it could be called that. Most of the recruits followed Pete and Dave down the forlorn main street to the Silver Dollar.

Inside the old, dark, lopsided saloon, the local clientele viewed this latest batch of olive-drabbed enthusiasm ambivalently. Recruits had been passing through Leadville to Camp Hale for seven months now, since December 1942. Several miners, denim overalls and course shirts revealing the hard labor of their profession, shook their creased, grimy faces, annoyed, compassionate, and inquisitive all at once.

After a little while one older soldier, who looked a bit weepy from either drinking too much liquor or going off to war—no one could tell —raised his glass in honorarium to America and to his father, and encouraged the other recruits to do likewise. They all stood, the weepy soldier said a few words, and they quickly downed their drinks. Dave drank his Coke. Pete stood as well, but he stared into his glass the whole time and swallowed his round before everyone else.

The shrill whistle of the D&RGW echoed through the streets of Leadville. The recruits dropped some crumpled bills on the bar and sprinted out the door and back up the street. They ran to the depot and were helped onto the ladder of the last car of the departing train by the outstretched arm of an older gentleman in a summer business suit.

Pete and Dave plopped down on opposite seats. They smiled at each other, catching their breath. Dave adjusted the precise knot of his tie and picked some invisible lint off his clean, crisp tunic.

"What's wrong,?" Pete asked.

"Nothing. I'm just a little disheveled from running around."

Dave bent over and retied the laces of his shoes, pulling them tight and making the loops as symmetrical as he could.

Pete pulled his cap over his eyes and tried to sleep. He woke up as the train slowed, struggling through a sooty tunnel as it dragged its passenger cars over Tennessee Pass. Their car swayed from side to side, reminding him of when he was a boy and in need of comfort, how his nanny would wrap her arms around him and rock him when he was frightened. He flashed a sad smile, almost certain he could still smell her lilac perfume. He always thought it was her he missed, but for the first time he realized that what he missed was being comforted, knowing he wasn't alone when he was frightened.

Does this mean I'm frightened now, God?

Dave nudged Pete with his shoe, grinning. "What are you smiling about? The Silver Dollar?"

"Yeah," Pete lied. "That place is chock-full of some real characters."

"I think one of those grimy miners wanted to challenge you to a drinking contest."

Pete nodded. "I'm sure you're right. Those guys are nuts."

Then he got up, lowered the window, and draped his arms and

head halfway out, concealing his face from Dave. Tears came. It was the first time he ever really prayed.

I think I'm afraid, God. I hope Lon was right when he told me years ago that You're not like my dad. If I matter to You, could You somehow show me that I'm not alone?

The D&RGW slowed, then came to a gentle stop at the depot on the northern end of the Pando Valley. Pete scrunched his nose as he got off. The air was clear, but it was overpowered with the smell of smoke from the train and the hundreds of barrack stoves. Laid out before him was Camp Hale. Pete squinted in the dazzling, high-altitude sunshine. As he tried to get his bearings, a sergeant yelled at the recruits to form up in a line with their duffel bags for the march to their barracks.

Quietly, Pete sang to Dave, "You're in the army now, you're not behind a plow . . ."

"Cool it, Pete. We don't need to get on some sergeant's shit list."

"Yeah, Dave, fine, whatever you say."

They marched in step as well as new recruits could, in a long, eager column, toward generic rows of low, white buildings. Pete guessed it was about seventy-five degrees, but he knew the sun's strength and the warmth of the air would evaporate with the day and that the cool, blue light of the hills, at dusk, would win out. Clouds of reddish dust billowed from the road as the men marched. Pete was directly behind Dave, who kept glancing down at his shoes. Pete looked down at the thick coat of pinkish dust that had gathered on his polished, brown, government-issue shoes. They marched on, Dave continuing his obsession with his shoes.

As they marched past the northern guardhouse and officially entered Camp Hale, the Eagle River bubbled on as it splashed along in its descent, down the middle of the camp. The burnt stench of the incinerator filled the air. Wispy, gray smoke crawled from its stack. The coal yard was just beyond—its black mounds a contrast of shimmering dustiness. The motor pool was close by. Somebody was cussing, and a wrench clanged around beneath the raised hood of a Willys Jeep. Next to it a deuce and a half sat partially hidden, its grill sticking out from the bay and the hood raised.

The line of recruits marched on, in heavy unison, guided by the rigid commands of a short, brawny drill instructor. Beyond the fire station and the pressing rows of whitewashed barracks, the steady pop of rifles punctuated the air, from a range somewhere in the distance to the south. Several men moved about, high up on a cliff. They were using a rope, but from the distance Pete couldn't tell if they were ascending or repelling down. He squinted in the glare of the sun and tried to get a better view of the rock climbers. The column was ordered to halt, but Pete hadn't noticed and bumped into Dave, knocking his duffel bag to the ground with a muffled thump. Dave attempted to retrieve the bag, but the short, brawny sergeant called them to attention beforehand.

"Damn it, you shitbags!" cursed their drill instructor. "What the hell is going on back there?! You better get it together if you expect to survive against the Third Reich longer than a session with your sweetheart! Now move out!"

They marched another hundred yards or so and made a crisp left turn at a street intersection bordered by identical buildings. The sergeant stopped them again halfway down the street, between more rows of nameless, pale living quarters and quickly, brusquely sorted them into their assigned barracks, but not before he informed them that they had precisely ten minutes to change into their fatigues and be lined up outside the mess hall for chow.

Pete and Dave were in the same building and shared a bunk together. Pete took the top bunk, changed quickly into drab fatigues and a white T-shirt, threw his duffel into his locker box, and tied his boots. He leaned against the top of the bunk, watching Dave sort his locker box.

"Dave, we're going to be late. You're going to make us late."

"I know, just a few more seconds. Hold on, I'm almost done."

"I'm going to dinner. We're in the sergeant's crosshairs already, and you're not helping."

Dave continued to sort his footlocker, moving fast and precisely now. He finished a moment later.

Pete turned and walked purposefully toward the door, his heavy boots clicking down the center of the now-empty barrack. Dave caught up to him.

Once outside, Pete checked his watch again and began to trot in the direction of where he thought the sergeant told them the mess hall lay. Then it came into view. A line of men had already formed and stood at attention. They waited for the sergeant's permission to enter. Pete and Dave scrambled toward the rear along with a few other stragglers. Pete glanced to his left and saw the sergeant's eyes tracking them.

"Damn you, Dave. He's eyeing us," Pete mumbled out of the corner of his mouth. "That's it. We're on his shit list."

"Sorry, Pete. Ten minutes wasn't enough time. You know how I get when I'm flustered. It only makes things worse. Besides, he doesn't recognize us from this distance. He doesn't know our faces yet. We're okay."

Pete lined up behind Dave. They were all at attention now, and the sergeant marched them into the chow hall.

As Pete and Dave moved past the sergeant, he yelled, "I'm watching you two knuckleheads! I'm going to be all over you if you're not careful. We'll kick both of your slacking asses right out those gates if you don't shape up."

Pete and Dave said nothing, walking past huddled rows of men gulping down their dinners. They headed toward a line of food with shiny bins and perspiring cooks draped in bleached aprons.

11 - COOPER HILL

Pete, Dave, and the rest of the men in their barracks stood at attention on the dirt road that ran through the main part of Camp Hale, just outside their billet. Dust wafted about in the still air while the sun's rays burrowed into their tanned faces. Sweat trickled down Pete's temples. He did his best to remain at attention while fidgeting under the load of his ill-adjusted pack. Its straps dug into his shoulders.

Sergeant Kirchoff, their drill instructor, informed them in a loud, I'm-doing-my-best-to-tolerate-you-idiots voice what their agenda would be for the next five days.

"I'm glad you sons of bitches finally decided to show up. Pay attention, ladies, 'cause you ain't worth me wasting my breath repeating myself. We're gonna march in a straight line up to the top of Tennessee Pass. We'll march for twenty-five minutes, rest for five minutes, and so on. Each time we break, grab something to eat. When we get there, we're gonna set up camp and hit the sack quick as shit through a goose. Then you're gonna get your sorry little asses up at 0500, make breakfast, grab an axe or a pick, along with your pack, and march up onto Cooper Hill. Then we're gonna spend the next three days clearing trees so that by the time Mother Nature shits her snowflakes on you, you'll have some nice, pretty little ski runs to train on. Move out!"

It was dark by the time the men reached Tennessee Pass's apex. They set up their pup tents, grabbed a quick bite of K-rations, then went to bed, an evening wind whipping about.

The next morning, in the predawn darkness, the men gobbled up some C-rations before forging their way up the east side of Tennessee Pass, packs on their backs and axes and picks in their hands. The sun was cresting the eastern ridges by the time they reached their designated area.

In teams of two, men chopped down a tree, lopped off the scores of its branches, then rolled it to the side, lining it up with hundreds of other trees the Eighty-Sixth Infantry Regiment had knocked down. Eventually someone would come by with one of the hundreds of Missouri mules the Tenth had in its possession, lash a chain around the trunk, affix it to the mule's harness, and haul it down the slope toward Highway 24.

It was the middle of the afternoon. Mount Massive and Mount Elbert lay to the west, their gray, brutish hulks hazy in the blue distance and the heat of the summer. Nearly all of their snow was gone, except for a few dingy couloirs where the snow was tainted red with the mud, dirt, and dust of summer. The peaks sat silently, passing the time until the familiar trappings of winter.

Pete's muscles ached and sweat poured off him, the veins in his tanned arms and the striations in his sunburned shoulders bulging from his labor. He stopped, removed his soaked undershirt, and nearly drained his canteen without pausing to take a breath. Then he called over his shoulder.

"Hey, Dave, I don't hear you chopping. Are you slacking on me?"

Pete turned around. Dave was staring at the Sawatch Range to the west, his hands resting on top of his axe handle and a peaceful smile on his face, like someone remembering a former lover.

"Dave, do you think we could scale them in the winter?"

"Huh?"

"Over there"—he pointed to the west—"Mount Elbert and Mount Massive. Do you think we could scale them in the winter?"

"Sure, why not? With skis and skins, I suppose we can climb most anything in the winter."

"We could start scouting routes as soon as the snow flies, Dave. We could head up there even before Halloween—you know, see what kind of snow is there and ski what we can. It'd be crappy conditions, but we'd be skiing, eh?"

A piney breeze gusted, and some camp robber birds dove nearby then swooped back up to their perches, cocking their heads as they rested on their perches. Farther up the woody ridge a tree crashed through its neighbors, smacking the ground with a deep, hollow thump.

"Pete, remember when you were a kid, and the barnstormers came through town?"

"The old aces of the Great War? Of course. Who doesn't?"

"Gosh, I loved those guys. I wanted to be Raoul Lufbery, you know, gunning it out with the Red Baron, somewhere over France. A Great War pilot even gave me a leather flying cap once, with goggles and everything. I ran all the way home with that stupid thing on."

"Do you still have it?"

Dave shook his head.

"What happened to it?"

"My dad got rid of it. He said being a pilot was foolish. He wanted me to be an engineer, have a stable profession. What did your dad want you to be?"

Just then a hawk rose into the sun, off to the left on an updraft. Silently it drifted south, in the direction of the broad, green valley of the Arkansas River beyond Leadville. The hawk circled, twisted its head, and seemed to have spotted something. It dove toward a flat outcropping of rock, gray and pink, mottled with bright green and orange lichen. Pete lost sight a moment, then the hawk emerged again. Its brown feathers glistened in the sun, and its screech echoed into the rock fissures and over the remnants of last winter's cornices. It had a snake in its talons now, probably a rattler, which writhed in futility, and it flew west until it dropped from sight over the dark green knobs on the west side of the pass.

"My dad never told me what he wanted me to be. He just expected me to go into the family business, the way his dad did with him, maybe like all dads."

"Didn't you want to know his thoughts about your future?"

"I suppose I did, but I grew tired of waiting, so I moved on."

The sun was growing stale, and the western ridges faded toward it. Further south a wall of gray moved in over La Plata Peak, and the rain pulled the sky down in wispy fingers that cleansed the high cirques of summer's muddy, gritty imprint.

Before long the supervising officers called it quits for the day, and the line of proud, hard, tired young men marched back down the ridge to their tents, warm sleeping bags, and cold rations. Pete, Dave, and the rest of their crew still had several days left in their timber-clearing shift before they would head back to Camp Hale.

Pete lay awake in his down sleeping bag inside the tent. The wind gusted and a burst of cold washed over his face, scented with the sweet aroma of the pines. He thought of the cold reaches of space, there between the stars. He felt small. And he thought of his dad who, he was sure, slept soundly under the same stars at this very moment, in a tidy stupor. He dreamt.

Pete was piloting a Sopwith Camel looking for the Red Baron. Dave was flying next to him in an identical plane. Dave wore a leather flying cap and goggles. He yelled to Pete to get his treasure chest out. Pete searched around his cockpit but found nothing. When he looked up, the Red Baron was flying next to him, and Dave was riding in the back, dressed in a German uniform. Pete watched as Dave reached down in the cockpit and hoisted up an enormous treasure chest. Then Dave emptied the chest over the side of Richtofen's red plane. Jewels, pearls, gold, and silver spilled out, and disappeared as they fell to earth. Then Dave jumped out also. He had no parachute, but as he fell he reached for a rope ladder that descended from the tail of the Red Baron's plane. He climbed down the ladder out of sight.

Pete jumped out of his plane also. He had no parachute either, and the ground spun as it approached him. He screamed, but the rushing wind drowned out his voice. He felt as though his breath was leaving his body. He couldn't feel his heartbeat. He hit the ground, but it had turned to water.

Now he was floating in Lake Erie, and luggage bobbed up and down nearby. A long, rusty freighter steamed by quickly. It almost ran over him. He yelled for someone on the deck of the ship to throw him a life preserver. The people on board either ignored him or didn't hear his call. There was an elegant party going on. The men were dressed in tuxedos, and the women wore gowns of silver, blue, white, and green. A band played jazz, and everyone sipped champagne and blew horns and yelled, "Happy New Year!"

Pete grabbed a suitcase that floated near him. It had a small, outboard motor attached to it. He started the motor and headed toward shore, away from the ship. As he neared the beach, he saw Dave sitting by a fire, dressed now in his army uniform. Dave was cooking something over the fire. No, actually he was baking something, on a large board with a long wooden handle. It was a loaf of bread. Pete landed on the beach, then walked up to Dave, who offered him a large hunk of bread. It was golden brown and crispy on the outside, steamy and fluffy on the inside, and Pete was desperately hungry. He tried to open his mouth but couldn't. He wept. Then Dave laughed and held up a golden key.

"Need this?" he said.

The next morning, while clearing more endless groves of pine trees, Pete described his dream to Dave.

"What do you think it was about?" Pete asked.

Dave continued to swing his axe, and Pete thought maybe he hadn't heard his question. Then Dave swung his axe extra hard into the trunk of a tree, where it sank in and stuck. Dave let go of the axe handle, pulled out his canteen from his rucksack, poured some water over his head, then took a gulp.

"There seems to be a lot of allegory in your dream. I'm not sure what it all may mean, but I'll tell you what I think. The treasure chest may represent the heart; the heart is where we hold our most cherished beliefs. So it's like the 'treasure' of our lives. According to your dream, you seem to see me as having many beliefs I hold dear, whereas you see yourself as not really having any beliefs that might be considered 'valuable.'

"The part about you landing in Lake Erie and being separated from the freighter, where the party was taking place, is probably a symbol of you breaking free from your old life.

"As for the last part, I think that's the most interesting piece, where I'm baking bread on the beach, and I have a golden key in my hand. God often portrays Himself as the Bread of Life in the Bible. It seems like there is some kind of deep, subconscious desire inside you, for God, which would make sense to me. I believe God puts this inside all human beings."

12 - THE TROOPER TRAVERSE

Six months later Pete and Dave huddled with a group of soldiers, thirty-three in all, and gazed across the frozen surface of Turquoise Lake, a few miles west of Leadville. A thick blanket of snow on the lake kept its secrets tucked away while a gale-force wind whipped across it. There was no hint of the day in the eastern sky, and it seemed the whole world slumbered.

Pete shifted uneasily; his ninety-pound rucksack and mountain tent rattled, and the snow beneath his skis was so cold that it squeaked. The best skiers at Camp Hale were selected to be instructors and formed the Mountain Training Group. It was this elite team that was "volunteered" to participate in a forty-mile expedition from Leadville to Aspen. Pete and Dave were part of this group, which was led by Captain John Jay and Sergeant Paul Petzoldt.

The platoon moved out again, skirted the lake, and headed north and west. Their pace was clumsy. Then they found their rhythm as the sky behind them began to shed the night.

Toward the end of the first day, beneath an overcast sky, the men trudged up to the drainage of Halfmoon Creek. They whisked through the last of the timberline, and bedded down in the forested crease between Mount Elbert and Mount Massive. The huge, rotting Champion Mill loomed nearby, rising out of the trees as though it strained to come back to life.

The next morning, when it was close to eleven o'clock, the leaden sky pressed in close as the group cleared the timberline, at 11,500 feet, and labored toward Mount Champion, still a way off. The wind picked up, and the snow seemed to swirl from above and below. Each man hugged the earth as best he could. The pace quickened.

Up on Darling Pass clouds engulfed everything and the wind howled ceaselessly. The pass was in an inhospitable mood. Pete hardly noticed a boulder—almost as large as a small house—that squatted at the top of the eastern lip of the pass. He labored by, then eased off his pace for a few moments, trying to catch his breath and recover some of his draining strength.

He called after Dave, who stopped and turned around, his face pinched and flushed.

"Dave, my whole stinkin' body hurts."

"I know. Me, too. Don't talk about it, Pete. Just keep moving."

The group began to huddle around Captain Jay on the west edge of the pass. Pete skied forward more eagerly now. He joined the rest of the men, who pressed in close to one another trying to conserve body heat. As the last man reached the group, Jay addressed the men.

"Men, we need to get off this pass fast and shelter in the trees but stay as close to the timberline as possible. Form up, keep your distance, and be alert."

The group spread out as each man bent down and secured the heel of his ski boots to his bindings. Captain Jay, followed by Sergeant Petzoldt, plunged over the side and disappeared from sight. One by one, each soldier did the same. As Pete dropped down the west side of the pass, icy air filled his lungs as he floated through cold, billowy, fathomless snow. It was tricky at first with his heavy pack. Then he recovered and began to enjoy himself. Down, down he glided as he made big, sweeping S-turns. He sat back on his skis and held his arms out to each side for balance. He cut through the light, smooth snow like an eagle riding the drafts.

About a thousand feet down Pete caught sight of Jay and Petzoldt as they veered toward a fairly large clump of conifers that darkened the crease between two sugary hills. Pete whisked into the glen, stopped next to Dave, took off his ninety-pound pack, and removed his skis.

He and Dave grabbed their shovels and set about, along with the rest of the men, digging out small, rudimentary sections of snow that they could shelter in while boiling water for soup and coffee and the rest of their C-rations. Pete, his undergarments damp with sweat, dug quickly.

At about one o'clock that afternoon, Captain Jay and Sergeant Petzoldt rousted the men from their snow shelters to continue the descent into the valley, toward Lake Creek's North Fork. Pete was stiff from inactivity, but grateful he'd changed into a dry pair of socks. He'd placed his sweaty pair of socks on the back of his neck, as he had been instructed, so that his body heat would dry them out while he ate. He and Dave gathered up their mess kits and cleaned them hastily with a few clumps of snow.

Everyone clipped into their ski bindings and struggled into the straps of their steel-framed packs. Within minutes the entire platoon was on its way, deeper down the North Fork Valley.

Pete skied clumsily, following the line of men in front of him. He couldn't find his rhythm. The snow was crusty on top, softer underneath. The tips of his skies rode above the crust briefly, then plunged underneath, then shot back up, and on and on. He dropped down into the blue valley. The wind from the speed of his descent whipped his wet clothing. He shook uncontrollably but pressed on, clumsy from his pack's weight. Breathing hard, he neared the bottom, and his legs felt like they were on fire, but he kept going, along with the rest of the men. Captain Jay and Sergeant Petzoldt didn't let up. Time seemed to speed up, the waning day urging the men on.

They gathered at the bottom of the valley. The North Fork creek was partially crusted, its banks extending over the river in a snow-covered, icy shelf. They spent a quarter of an hour looking for a spot to cross where the ice and snow had created a natural footbridge. They found one, trudged across in anxious movements, and climbed through the pine groves on the west side of the valley, making for the Continental Divide beyond.

The expedition cleared the trees and moved higher up. Pete

stopped for a moment, but Jay and Petzoldt kept going. Plodding, they angled for a saddle still hundreds of feet up, working in switch-back fashion without pause. Pete grunted loudly, then moved on. Dave was behind him, the rhythm of his tired, labored breaths matching his own.

Pete cleared the wind-blown lip of the saddle and skied toward an enormous flat of rock a few hundred yards west. The officers had decided to break camp there, and Pete watched intermittently as the cold sun broke through a low line of sodden clouds before dipping behind Mount Champion.

Pete neared the rock. Some men threw off their packs, removed their skis, and assembled their stoves on the rock slab. Others began digging shallow pits in the snow for the tents. It was no longer snow-ing, but the wind felt fiercer and more remorseless. Pete tried to forget his discomfort, focusing only on the many tasks now at hand.

He threw off his pack and unclipped his skis. He stripped off the damp layers from his upper body. The wind lashed his skin. He shook hard, and dug furiously through his backpack for his dry, extra shirt of long underwear. He found it and covered himself in a flash. He put the rest of his layers back on and left them unbuttoned, hoping they'd dry out somehow in the dreary wind. His socks were another matter.

Pete grabbed his shovel, marched a few paces from the rock, and dug. He carried the tent, so he decided he would prepare the sleeping quarters while Dave, carrying their small stove, would fix something to eat. The snow was thick and crusty on the surface, somewhat lighter underneath, but still lousy.

Dave skied up. His breathing had returned to normal, but his movements were slow and wooden.

"What gives?" Dave said.

"Tents on the snow, stoves on the rock…makes sense. This snow is worthless. I figured I'd work on this and let you worry about dinner, since you have the stove and all."

"Affirmative."

"How are you doing?"

Dave shrugged.

"You look tired, Dave. You're not winded, but you're moving like you're really worn out. Have you got some dry clothes and socks?"

"Yeah."

"Good. You better change into those before you get the stove fired up."

"Sure but, hell, it's going to take a while to melt enough snow for any decent amount of water for cooking, Pete. We may have to settle for cold C-rations."

"I was afraid you'd say that."

Dave changed into a dry undershirt as well, and put on his dry pair of socks. He assembled their stove, made sure to set up the wind-break, packed an aluminum cup full of snow, and set it on the burner. With difficulty, he lit the burner with his Zippo. Ten minutes later Dave had melted all the snow in his cup, but it only yielded a couple of inches of water. He grabbed his canteen and shook it hard. The ice inside broke apart and sloshed around. He was about to pour the frigid water into the metal cup but changed his mind, turned off the stove, and packed it back up.

At the same time, Pete measured out a small area for their tent. The snow was up to his knees. He dug through the upper crust to the softer snow beneath and stopped about halfway down. Then he put his skis on and stomped on the remaining snow, packing it down as best he could. This warmed him up, and took off a few layers. He trudged over to the rock slab and grabbed the alpine tent.

"No hot chow for dinner, Dave?"

"I gave up on the idea. It'll take way too long. C-rations for dinner and let's get some shut-eye."

"Okay. Can you give me a hand with the tent?"

Ten minutes later Pete and Dave had their tent set up, with their double-down sleeping bags inside. Pete grabbed a can of C-rations and devoured cold beans and chunks of a frankfurter. The rest of the platoon began to bed down. The sky was slate again, cheerless.

Lying in their sleeping bags, waiting for sleep to take hold, Dave spoke.

"Lucy's been sick lately, Pete."

"What's wrong?"

Dave shrugged. "The doctors don't know, at least not yet."

"Aw, Dave, I'm sorry. When did all this happen?"

"Within the last month."

"Why didn't you tell me?"

"I didn't want to burden you. You've got your own problems to worry about."

"Dave, friends are supposed to bear each other's burdens."

"It's okay, Pete. It seems like they caught it quick. I talked to Lucy on the phone. She said the doctors sound optimistic."

"Did she sound optimistic?"

"I'm not sure."

The wind whipped the tents' fabric to and fro, up and down, like the staccato of a machine gun. They slid into their double sleeping bags and passed out as the snow started to drive in. Pete's mind wandered through the night.

He was in a lodge, high in the Alps. There was a terrible snowstorm outside, and the snow had piled up so high that the windows of the lodge were almost completely obscured. It was getting very dark inside. Pete was playing chess with an officer in the German army. The officer had a trim mustache, peaked cap, monocle, and gold braiding down the side of his gray breeches, which were tucked into his black riding boots. He had gloves on and a riding crop tucked under his arm.

Pete said, "Maybe I should go outside and clear some of the snow away from the windows."

The officer said, "If you go out into the storm, you will most surely die. I know about these storms. They can easily kill a man. And besides, you cannot continue our game if you get caught up in the storm."

"But, Colonel, soon the storm will make it impossible to keep on playing."

"Nonsense! You must stay calm. Let the storm worry about itself. We have light in here as well."

The officer lit a cigar, which glowed with a pale, bluish light. The light grew brighter until it filled the entire room. Pete resumed his chess match.

There was a rapid, hard knock at the door. Pete glanced at the door, then at the officer, who waved it off with his gloved hand. They kept playing, but the knocks grew louder and more frequent, and then turned into a series of scrapes, like a long knife searching for a crack in the door that could be pried open.

Just beyond the heavy door a muted voice called out. Pete was sweating. Pete heard his name called.

"That's Dave, Colonel! He's trying to get in."

"You must not open the door."

"But Dave will freeze to death."

"He will kill you if you let him in. Do not open the door."

"He is my friend."

"You must protect the game. Focus! Hurry now, swallow the chess pieces."

Pete devoured all the black chess pieces, then all the white ones. His stomach hurt. Then the scraping at the door turned into a banging, a shoulder being rammed into the thick wood. The wood began cracking, the joints separating.

"Hurry!" yelled the officer. "We must guard the game!"

The officer grabbed a long knife, almost as long as a bayonet. It gleamed from the fire in the hearth, and its handle was ivory, with a small silver eagle on top. The officer rushed toward the door, and Pete, laden with his combat gear, grabbed his knife as well and followed the German. His legs couldn't move forward very well. He couldn't run. The officer screamed at him again, and he flung the door of the lodge open. A frigid blast of snow and wind engulfed Pete, and then the German hit him full force in the back, and his face slammed into the floor of the porch. He heard Dave's voice as he was being dragged across the floor. He was flung into the snow and cold outside, and vomited.

· · ·

Pete jolted awake and sat up inside his tent. His sleeping bags constricted his movements. It was black. There was only the wind and Dave's snoring. His stomach gnawed at him.

He reached inside his down bag and pulled out his canteen. His mouth felt like cotton, and the frigid water, already chunky with ice, was welcome. He reached down inside his bag again and pulled out a candy bar. It was gone in two bites, crammed in his mouth. His thoughts turned toward his dad and then to Dave's World War I flying cap.

I wonder what my dad would've said if I'd come home with one? Dad probably wouldn't have said anything. He'd have just stared at me, then gotten up from his leather office chair and checked the ticker.

He thought of his mom, too, with her lady friends and their cocktails and endless gossip. He lay back down, bit his nails, and tried to think of Aspen and the Hotel Jerome, where a steak and an "Aspen crud," the hotel's famous drink, awaited him. He fell asleep a long time later.

Sergeant Petzoldt's voice bellowed, rousting the men. Pete opened his eyes to discover it was still almost too dark to see. Dave stirred. The walls of the tent leaned inward.

Pete tried to stretch out the night's stiffness, but his sleeping bag confined him. He wiggled out, welcoming the cold rush of air. He stretched his shoulders and neck, and worked his legs back and forth, pumping the blood. Pots and stoves clanged outside.

In a sandpaper voice Pete said, "Dave, it's time to get up."

A muffled voice shot back, "I told the front desk not to give me a wake-up call."

"It snowed last night—a lot."

"No kidding, Pete? I hear it does that in the mountains."

"Let's get moving, Dave. We need to fire up the stove. I'd really like some coffee and hot oats."

Pete added layers of wool clothing while Dave creaked out of his sleeping bag, moaning. Then Pete grabbed their stove, left the tent, and walked toward a cluster of fellow soldiers to make breakfast.

A short while later Dave walked back to the tent, carrying oats, several C-rations of peaches, and some instant coffee. They made breakfast quickly, ate even faster, then packed up their tent and gear and moved out as though they were under fire.

Jay and Petzoldt led the group west again. The Continental Divide loomed above, its granite mass thrust into the searing blue sky. The troopers avoided a steep avalanche slope, an apron to a high pass, and angled lower for a different, safer pass further west. The platoon glided on their white skis, the sun at their backs, as they traversed a ragged highline next to the head of Lost Man Creek. Captain Jay wasted no time, plunging down into the drainage. One by one his men followed suit. Intemperate and untamed, each man used his skis to create his own work of art on the blank canvas of snow.

They drove on, still westward, up the next ridge. Williams Mountain gaped ahead, a sharp picket line of brutish, gray rock and deep, snowy couloirs. The group stopped and huddled around Jay and Petzoldt, conferring and debating about the safest route down toward Hunter Creek's headwaters. They shifted on their skis and scanned the jagged peaks for a way across.

Pete removed his pack; the cold air refreshed his back and shoulders. He sipped from his canteen, tried to eat something, and made a witty comment to Dave, who didn't respond but instead stared at the rocky wall that thwarted their advance.

Captain Jay and Sergeant Petzoldt decided to send out two-man patrols to scout Williams Mountain for the safest route the platoon could descend. Dave volunteered himself and Pete for one of the patrols.

Six pairs of scouts trudged west-northwest through dry snow that reached the top of their shins. As Pete followed Dave's tracks, he felt the hard base of old snow beneath the night's latest arrival. Somewhere in his thoughts was the notion that this could be a portent of disaster. He brushed it off, focusing instead on staying warm and looking for a safe route down to Hunter Creek.

Dave and Pete approached a long, broad bluff that from a distance looked like a thick, white blanket tucked right up under a craggy, gnarled ridge. As they got closer, they could see a narrow gap that broadened into something resembling a canyon and an exit.

Dave was about twenty meters ahead of Pete. He stopped and peered over an edge. Pete skied up, gliding silently through the upper layer of snow while his skis crunched on the one underneath.

"What's up?"

"Looks dicey. You've got a heck of a cornice here and a pretty steep couloir below."

Pete moved gingerly to the edge and gazed below. He whistled. "Wow, that's steep. At least it's not all rocks."

It seemed like a decent amount of snow lay down below. Most likely, the chute had the most amount of snow they'd find on such steep gullies.

"You could be right," Dave said, "but this cornice is a heck of a drop. We're talking about building up some serious speed with our packs and all. We'd hit the chute like a rocket, with hardly any room to maneuver, and there are sharp rocks on either side. 'Dicey' is putting it mildly."

"Let's see what the others have found, Dave. All I'm saying is that this may be the only gully with enough snow to ski down. How 'bout if I wait here while you go back and report what we've found? If somebody thinks they've discovered a better way down, then you can wave me over, but all the same, I'd just as soon wait here and maybe scout this couloir a little more and see if I can find the best line down."

Dave gave him a long look. "Don't get any wild ideas and go skiing down this thing alone."

"Yes, dear." Pete hated it when Dave seemed to know what he was thinking.

"Dang it, I'm serious! You know there's no room for goofing off up here."

"Relax. I'll wait on you and the captain and the rest of the men." He knew he should be grateful that Dave cared about his safety, but it irked him being talked to like a child.

"All right, I'll be back in a jiffy." Dave pulled out a small tin and rubbed zinc oxide on his lips.

In the distance, Pete saw Dave pointing and waving. He looked comical, even desperate. Hot from the snow's reflection, Pete turned his back on the sun and the saddle, moving closer to the edge of the cornice. He peered down again, then moved north and west along its edge. The gully was shaded, and rocks, jumbled beneath a canopy of snow, framed the chute. It brought to mind some kind of sacred and forbidden place, another world, waiting in the half-light for the next day.

He heard Dave's voice, and when he looked over his shoulder, his friend was skiing rapidly toward him, the rest of the platoon in tow. Dave waved one of his ski poles at Pete who couldn't make out his words. Probably he wanted him to wait there, on the cornice, until he got there with everyone else.

Pete was certain the chute he and Dave had discovered was the route the platoon would choose to take to Hunter Creek and on to Aspen. He stood there in the sun, feeling strong on his skis, ready for the challenge as Dave, now halfway between him and the saddle, was shouting something.

Pete smiled with zinc-coated lips and nodded, looking every bit the expert. He waved Dave and the rest of the men onward with a zealous, upward arc of his bamboo ski pole. They seemed to take forever.

Deciding not to wait for them, Pete dropped over the edge of the cornice, into the shade, into the chute, suspended in the air. Still accelerating when he hit the snow, he collapsed, his heavy pack pressing into his back. His face smashed into his knees, and he tumbled. Snow stung his face. His skis and poles scattered, and his backpack slid up onto his head. He splayed his arms to halt his momentum, but the pitch was too steep, and he was sliding too fast on the snow. He careened into a heap of rocks, bashing his knee and the side of his head. When he came to a rest, his glasses were askew, and his hat, poles, and skis were scattered across the couloir.

Dazed, his temple and knee throbbing, Pete slid his pack off and crawled across the chute, gathering his equipment. When gazing back up the gully, to the edge of the cornice, he saw no one. He exhaled in relief and rubbed his jabbing knee. Carefully he touched the side of his head, then examined his ski glove. No blood, but he felt a huge lump.

If he put on his gear and skied over to his pack, he'd be ready to go by the time the others reached the cornice. No one would be the wiser.

Pete grabbed his poles and strapped on his skis. As he balanced the best he could on the chute's angle, he glided over to his pack, which lay on the snowy rocks. After it was on his back once more, he glanced up to the cornice. The men weren't there yet. He quickly turned himself around, precisely swung his skis so they were facing toward the center of the couloir, parallel, and waited.

Nuts, my goggles! Where are my goggles?

They still hung from his neck. Relieved, he placed them back on. Then Dave's voice echoed from the top of the gully.

"Hey, Pete, what the hell?! Why didn't you wait for us?! Stay there, I'm coming down!"

Dave eased over the edge of the cornice, then went into a free fall. He hit the chute with a *thwack*. Slabs of snow exploded in every direction as Dave's legs fought for control. Arms flailing, he made quick, frantic turns before coming to a stop just above Pete.

Sweat appeared on Pete's upper lip. He knew he was about to be scolded.

"What the hell is wrong with you, Pete?! Why didn't you wait like we planned?"

He struggled for words. "I guess I got a little impatient. Sorry, man."

"Saying sorry doesn't always fix everything!"

Pete hung his head in shame and wished he knew what else to say. He only nodded in quiet agreement.

Moments later voices echoed down the gully, sailing from above. Dave shouted up, briefing the first few men, coaching them over the cornice. The rest followed their lead. Soon a dozen soldiers were strung out, all the way up the shaded gully.

"Lead us out of here, Pete, before we get more backed up," Dave said.

Pete moved out, and Dave followed. Pete's turns were controlled, sluggish; his knee hurt, and he favored it. He was a hundred meters farther down now, but still Dave was close behind, and the men in the gully thinned out.

Suddenly the snow beneath Pete gave way. He fell fast into a cold darkness.

Below him, Dave landed first, onto a mere sliver of a rock ledge. Pete landed partially on top of him, his left leg bent back underneath him, trapped by his ski. Something in his knee popped, but he only had a moment to worry about it before he bounced off Dave and began to slip off the ledge. He struggled to hold on. His gloved hands caught a decent handhold on the lip of the ledge, but it couldn't last. His pack tugged at him, pulling him closer to the abyss below. He hung there, his legs dangling back and forth, skis still attached, while his poles fell away.

Help me, God! he thought, but "Shit!" was all that came out.

Arms quivering and teeth clenched, he managed to pull himself up, slow and determined. But his strength began to fail. The ledge was close. He launched himself back onto it, grasping wildly, and clutched Dave's stretched-out legs. He collapsed on top, breathing hard, eyes shut.

A few moments later he opened his eyes and managed to roll over. His comrades, lining the rim of the hole he'd fallen through, peered down at him. He spoke a few sentences to Dave before he realized Dave was unconscious.

"Private McGregor! What the hell happened?" Pete heard someone yell down.

"Hang on, ya moron!" His voice bounced off the sheer rock walls, cold and hollow.

"McGregor, it's Captain Jay here. Are you all right?"

Do I look all right?

"Sorry, sir, I didn't know it was you. Give me a minute, Captain."

Pete wasn't sure what to do.

Damn this rucksack! I wish I could ditch this thing.

Pete managed to get the rest of his body up on the ledge, wrestled his arms free of his pack, and shoved it against the rock wall. He turned around clumsily, and leaned against the wall, Dave's legs tucked under his own. The lower part of his legs hung over the ledge, his skis still attached. His knee throbbed and swelled. His comrades stared down at him, the flappy Tenth Mountain Division caps perched on top of their heads. Pete was cold and damp now.

"You guys gonna get us out of here, or did you want to snap some pictures instead?" Pete yelled.

Jay yelled back, "We'll get you out. Just hang on. Give me a situation report on you and your fellow soldier. Who is that with you?"

"Private Bates, sir."

"Okay. What's your status?"

"My knee is banged up, sir, and I'm getting pretty chilled down here. Give me a second and I'll check on Bates."

Pete leaned toward Dave and tried to examine his friend as best he could. He could see Dave's chest rise and fall slightly. Blood trickled down Dave's face from a dark, matted spot in his hair. He shook Dave. Nothing. Pete's throat tightened as panic seized him. Hands shaking, he grabbed his canteen, almost dropped it over the edge, then poured some into his hand and splashed it in Dave's face. His vision blurred as tears welled up. He shook him again, called out his name, then clapped his hands together inches above Dave's face.

"Dave! Dave! Wake up, buddy. Come on, Dave, talk to me."

Slowly Dave began to revive. He blinked his eyes, rubbed his face. He reached up to the bloody spot on his head and let out a yelp.

"Is that you, Pete?"

"Yeah, Dave, it's me. How do you feel?"

"Terrible."

"You took a pretty serious whack to your head, but I'm glad you're conscious. And you need to stay conscious. Can you sit up?"

"I think so. Give me a hand."

Pete helped him sit upright and remove his pack, then yelled up to Captain Jay that Dave was conscious but bleeding.

"Okay, McGregor, just hang on for a little bit, and we'll get you out quick as a flash and down to Aspen. Just hang on, and keep him awake."

"Yes, sir!"

They sat in silence, listening to the distant voices above. Lost in thought, it was a while before Pete checked his watch. "Geez," he mumbled to himself, "it's been over half an hour. What the hell are they doing up there?"

It was colorless in the crevasse, scoured and empty. It was, however, warmer than up on the snow, the earth venting itself through the fissure. The shaft of light from above spilled down and disappeared into the depth below.

Captain Jay shouted down to both men, saying they were ready to bring them out and tossed down one end of a hemp rope. It landed in a clump next to Pete. He fashioned a harness with it, placed it over Dave's head and threaded Dave's arms through it. He jerked on the rope, signaling for the platoon to haul Dave to the surface, to safety.

At the hole's opening the men grasped Dave and yanked him out. A short time later the rope flopped down again, back onto the ledge. Pete balanced on his good leg, put the improvised harness on, yanked on the rope, and watched the abyss recede as he was pulled to the light above, and to freedom.

The royal-blue sky was giving way to the violet hues before night. A quick, improvised travois was made for both Pete and Dave from the two extra mountain tents. The group threaded its way down the rest of the gully and made it to the start of Hunter Creek. Then they proceeded further into the trees, where they camped their final night.

Pete and Dave had a long, restless night filled with pain. But they survived, and the men towed them the rest of the way to Aspen. They spent the next week in the hospital before being taken back to Camp Hale, where they spent two more weeks in the infirmary.

13 - ON BELAY

Once Pete and Dave were both healed, the months of training dragged on. Pete began not sleeping well, anxious that Dave still wasn't proficient enough at rock climbing. He was afraid Dave would be a liability in combat. He brought this to the attention of his climbing instructor, David Brower. Brower responded, "I'm fully aware of Dave's deficiencies, Pete, so I'm pairing up the two of you because you *are* a good climber. I want you to help get him up to snuff."

One particular day in early May of 1944, Pete and Dave were climbing on the rock cliffs just to the east of Camp Hale, training for war, along with the other men of the Tenth Mountain Division. Along with skiing, rock climbing was a skill the men were required to master. Though the war was in its fifth year, the Tenth had yet to enter combat because the leaders in the War Department couldn't decide exactly where to use them.

The two friends were a few hundred feet above the valley floor, on the upper portion of a climb. Patches of snow and ice lay in the couloirs and on the shaded ledges of the cliffs. In the distance, Camp Hale's white buildings dazzled in the sunlight.

Dave led the climb, moving up the rock face methodically while Pete belayed him from down below. Dave had already wasted a lot of effort struggling to find the right pieces of gear on his improvised harness while maintaining his balance on razor-thin ledges and tiny knobs of rock.

Pete craned his neck as Dave came to the final section of the climb. It had a wall on the left side that ran less than halfway to the top of the pitch, rising about sixty feet with a few tiny ledges and several cracks. On the right there was a vertical crack rising 150 feet up, all the way to the top. The crack seemed an odd width to Pete, and it worried him.

Boy, that's a tricky section. That goofy crack is too wide for a piton or even a hand, but it looks like it's too narrow to jam a shoulder into. I hope Dave is all right.

"Dave, it looks like you're really going to have to search for those piton placements. The hardest portion, I think, will be the first one. Remember that if you fall before that first placement, you'll hit the deck down here."

"I'm aware of the danger."

Pete's neck ached from looking upward. He dropped his head, massaged his neck, and looked up again. Dave looked good for the first ten feet or so, then seemed to slow too much. He eventually found the initial piton placement, about twenty-five feet up. He pulled out his hammer and firmly tapped the piton into the fissure. Next, he placed a snap ring and attached the rope.

"Nice work, Dave."

Dave moved up the crack. He tried to jam his boot sideways into it, but it was too awkward. He crammed his hand in the crack and brought his boot underneath, wedging it in. He tested the placement with his weight, then slid his arm further up once his weight held. Like a human inchworm, he worked his way up, leaning back each time he had his hand in the crack in order to rest. Even far below, Dave's steady, labored breathing was audible.

Dave climbed another thirty feet. With his body contorted and an arm and a foot jammed in the fissure, Dave half twisted and yelled down over his shoulder.

"Whaddya think, Pete?"

"Scour the rock just above you, Dave. Look closely for any little opening you can ram a piton into."

"I don't know if I can pull this off. I'm tired."

"Come on, Dave. You've come all this way. Focus and work through this. There's no going back."

Dave inched his way up the crack again. He scanned the rock. With one hand and one foot wedged into the rock, he quickly reached for a piton, found it, and jammed it temporarily into a tiny crack. When he let go to reach for his hammer, the piton fell out, bonked him on the head and dropped away. Pete watched carefully and ducked out of the way of the falling piton, which clanked onto the rock beside him, caromed off, and bounced further down the pitch.

Dave reached for another piton and wedged it back, more carefully yet more forcefully this time, into the same crack. He deftly grabbed his hammer and rammed the piton firmly in place in four strokes. He clipped in and dropped his head down, resting it against the rock.

"On belay?" Dave called out.

"Belay on," Pete replied, letting Dave know he was ready with the rope secure.

Able to relax now, Dave pulled his arm and leg out of the crack and dangled from the hemp rope as it stretched slightly under his weight. He twisted lazily in the air.

"Come on, Dave, keep moving! You won't have time to rest with the Krauts shooting at you."

Dave wedged himself back in and inched up the crack once again.

"You're not too far from the top. I think a few more pitons should get you there."

"Okay."

Dave kept moving, made it about forty feet up, and placed his next piton and ring. Then, twenty feet higher up, he set his next to last placement.

"Okay, Dave, that's it. You can do this! Relax now, find your rhythm, and use only the muscles you need."

Ten feet from the top Dave finally found the last placement for a piton. He reached for one, quickly rammed it into the rock, reached again for his hammer, and knocked it in with three strokes. He snapped his ring into place, grabbed a section of rope, placed it in his teeth, reached down and grabbed some more, and finally clipped the rope in. He rested again.

Thirty seconds later he scaled the last section of rock. He was five feet from the top, while Pete carefully played out the rope 150 feet below. The crack narrowed and Dave jammed both hands inside, clenching them so that his knuckles wedged themselves against the rock. He leaned to the left, leveraging more pressure on his hands. He could virtually touch the top. He was in an awkward position, but he was almost there. Then he lost his hold.

By the time he'd fallen below his highest-placed piton, Pete, watching him closely, had already taken up the slack in the rope, which caused Dave to jerk momentarily as the rope straightened, stretched a bit, then tensed. Dave hung there.

But the respite lasted just a few seconds as the piton gave way and Dave plummeted an additional forty feet. There was no pause as Dave's momentum yanked the next piton out of the rock like a sling-shot. Knowing there was no way he had the time to take up the slack in the rope using the conventional approach, Pete dropped the rope he'd gathered and instead pulled hard and fast, hand over hand, gobbling up the yards of excess rope Dave's fall created. Pete didn't even look up, knowing Dave was in the midst of a deadly fall.

Dave fell another forty feet, and the next piton ejected violently from the rock as well. Still helpless, Dave dropped thirty-five more feet down to his lowest placement. He had free-fallen over a hundred feet. The last piton managed to hold. It was sixty feet above the ground, but Pete hadn't taken up all the remaining slack, and Dave fell past the placement, dropping another fifteen feet before the rope tensed, stretched, and bounced Dave to a jerky stop forty-five feet above Pete.

In the fall, Dave banged his head hard on the rock. Blood flowed freely from the top of his head and spread down his face. He dangled from the rope like a marionette, unconscious.

"Dave! Dave! Can you hear me? Nuts! Hang on, Dave, I'll get you down!"

Pete lowered Dave down smoothly and rapidly. Dave collapsed in a jumble on the sandstone. Pete splashed water on him, and he revived.

Pete helped him sit up and leaned him back against the rock, facing him to the sun.

Blood still oozed down Dave's face, drying dark red in parts but flowing bright red in others. He sat silently as Pete examined his wound and applied a field dressing to his head.

"You scared the shit outta me. Maybe this is one of those surface head wounds that look worse than they really are."

Dave stared vacantly as Pete finished wrapping his head.

"You ready to head out, buddy? We'll just walk it back to Hale, nice and easy, okay?"

"Not yet, Pete. Let me sit for just a little while."

The two friends sat on a level piece of rock, listening to the shouts and banter of their comrades, who were also training nearby, hidden among the rocks. A cool breeze of pine mixed with sage kicked up and washed over their faces. An eagle took flight from a tree branch and rode the currents west and south over Camp Hale, its head darting left and right, looking for food. Pete pulled out his canteen and sipped some water, then passed it to Dave, who drank long. Water trickled down his chin. He passed the canteen back to Pete, who grabbed it slowly and stared at Dave as he screwed the top back on then put it away. Both men sat for a while longer.

The faded, western hills were hazy in the sunlight now as the day neared its end. A distant, shrill wail far to the south announced the emergence of the D&RGW from the tunnel that ran under Tennessee Pass, the train chugging north toward Hale.

"Let's head back, Pete. It's getting cool, and my head is throbbing."

"Okay, but wait here a moment while I get a couple other guys to help get you down to camp."

Pete hustled over to a nearby rock face and solicited the help of two other comrades. Together they helped Dave to his feet. They walked back to Camp Hale in silence, the spring sun already behind the peaks, igniting the western sky in pink hues, then orange, and finally red.

The wind picked up in the Pando Valley as the men of the Tenth bedded down for another cold night, anxious that the war would end before they had a chance to fight.

14 - FALL OUT

In late May 1944, a few months after the Tenth completed its grueling D-series war games during a three-week period in an unseasonably frigid March, Dave came to Pete one day in the barracks just before lunch. He held a telegram in his hands. Both men sat on a lower bunk, an olive drab blanket wrapped tight around each bed with the ends tucked in immaculately.

"Is it about Lucy's polio?"

Dave nodded without looking up.

"How bad?" Pete whispered.

In a raspy, tear-choked voice, Dave said, "She only has a few weeks now."

Suddenly Dave scrunched the telegram in his hand, stood, and turned and buried his face in the rough wool blanket on the top bunk, grief erasing his composure.

Then, for the first time, God spoke to Pete in his thoughts, though at first he wasn't sure who it was.

Let go of your selfish ways, Peter.

Pete stood up and glanced around the room, certain another soldier was talking to him. There was no one else there. He grew dizzy, and suddenly felt as though he'd stepped out of his body and was staring at himself. Before he realized it, he stepped toward Dave, a hand on his shoulder as he stroked his hair in an awkward yet tender moment.

By late afternoon Dave and Pete had passes and were on their way to Denver by bus, since it would be faster than by train. It took a lot of convincing for both men to persuade their superior officers to let Pete accompany Dave. Eventually they relented.

Their bus ground its way up and over Vail Pass, then Loveland Pass, and snaked east, following Clear Creek. They passed aspens that shook their leaves like a hurrah for the coming of summer. The troops on the bus were wearing their dress uniforms. They smoked and bullshitted nonstop as they whipped up their enthusiasm for a weekend of skirt chasing, rounds of drinks, and other adventures.

It was almost nine o'clock in the evening by the time the bus reached the Brown Palace and all the men, Pete and Dave included, got off and checked into the hotel. In their shared room, Pete stood in front of a mirror and checked his hair while he adjusted his cap and tie. Dave sat on the edge of the bed.

Pete took a deep breath. "Ready to go to the hospital, Dave?"

Dave shrugged, averting his eyes from Pete. "Not much choice, is there?"

Pete was about to respond, but couldn't get the words out. Or was it that he didn't want to? Something inside told him it would dishonor Dave. Suddenly he felt selfish and ashamed.

Then they left the room and rode the elevator to the lobby in silence.

God, Pete prayed silently, *You know I'm no good at this. But Dave really needs You right now. Just…just carry his burden or whatever it is You do for people who are desperate. Amen.*

At the hospital Pete bought a bouquet of flowers in the lobby and took them to Lucy. She greeted him cordially and thanked him for the flowers. He made small talk, saying he was glad to see her, along with a few other lies. Then he wished her well, excused himself, and plopped into a chair just outside the door. He realized he was sweating, and loosened his tie.

A while later Pete heard a muffled, exasperated exchange of words. The crescendo came when Dave yelled.

"What do you *want* from me, Lucy?"

"Your heart, David! I've *always* wanted your heart."

It was quiet in the room after that. Then Pete heard more muffled conversation. A long time passed. He exchanged awkward glances with an attractive redhead behind the nurses' station desk in the hall across from Lucy's room.

"I guess it's not going too well in there, is it?"

"It doesn't sound like it, soldier. I'm sorry."

Pete nodded grimly and fumbled with his service cap.

The nurse smiled sympathetically. "Well, I'm sure he's glad he has a friend with him."

Pete stared blankly at her, thinking about what she'd said. Something about her face looked trustworthy and kind. "I don't think I've been a good friend to him," he blurted out. "I act so selfish sometimes. I don't know why I do that." His eyes seemed to plead for an answer. Then he turned away. "I'm sorry for sharing this with you. It's inappropriate for strangers, I know."

Pete looked up, startled by the sound of heels clicking on the linoleum floor of the hallway. The nurse stood before him, a delicate hand on his shoulder.

"It's never too late to change direction," she whispered, then walked back to her desk.

Before Pete could respond, Dave appeared from Lucy's room abruptly and closed the door with some force. His eyes found Pete, and he glared at him.

"Come on, Pete, let's get moving."

Pete turned to the nurse. "Thank you." A quick smile. "I hope you're right."

They rode in silence on the elevator. Pete stood just behind Dave's shoulder, watching him. Dave mumbled to himself, Pete catching a curse word here and there.

They reached the first floor, the doors opened, and they walked out into an overcast September day. Soldiers and other men and women in uniform passed them. A streetcar clamored by, followed by a couple of trucks and a taxi. Dave looked up as though he was searching for words. They headed toward the Brown Palace, and still Dave said nothing.

Pete broke the silence. "It didn't sound like it went too well in there, Dave. I'm really sorry."

Dave's pace slowed. Hands in his trouser pockets, he talked while he stared at the sidewalk.

"God has His reasons, Pete. But, damn, He makes it so difficult sometimes."

"He makes what difficult?"

Dave stopped suddenly and looked Pete in the eye. "Trusting Him."

They walked in silence the rest of the way to the hotel. Ten days later Lucy died. Dave was by her side. Pete and a few other soldiers traveled down to Denver for the funeral. The next day they were back at Camp Hale, training and wondering if they'd get their chance to fight.

The next month, in June 1944, Pete, Dave, and the rest of the men in the Tenth were told the entire division was being transferred to Camp Swift in Texas, to boost its complement of men and beef up its equipment. Morale in the division plummeted, as this meant mountain soldiers being forced onto the hot, humid flatlands.

On a sweltering day in a landscape flat, brown, and barren as far as the eye could see, Pete and Dave practiced their marksmanship at the rifle range. The loud pops from the M1s and carbines mixed with the whir of machine gun bursts from the Thompsons and BARs created a wall of noise.

When they were done and had some free time, they walked to the PX, the camp's general store. Dave fumbled with his T-shirt, pulling it away from his body to try to cool off.

"So what do you think, Dave? Will we ever get into the war?"

A platoon ran past them in two columns as the drill instructor kept the cadence, barking out his commands and leading the troops' singing. They kicked up a choking dust, scores of boots in unison. Pete walked on and didn't give it much notice. Dave swatted at the filthy air.

"Hard to say. From what I've heard, the army brass in DC aren't sure where to place us. We're the only division of its kind, so wherever they commit us, it needs to be a perfect fit."

Pete nodded and opened the door to the PX, its whitewashed surface blistering and peeling. He and Dave each bought a bottle of Coke. Pete nursed the welcomed soda. Dave chugged his Coke until it was empty, even before they reached the exit. Dave turned around and purchased another. Then they headed back the way they had come. Pete lagged behind, his hands deep in his pockets.

Halfway to the rifle range Pete slowed his steps, then grabbed Dave by the arm.

"Dave, I need to ask you something. How come you never talk about Lucy?"

"It's private, Pete. It's between me and God."

Pete nodded, and they walked on. Moments later Pete stopped him again.

"Dave, I'm sorry, I know you said Lucy's death is a private matter, but we're best friends. Surely it's eating you up inside, right?"

Dave's eyes narrowed, and he pressed his lips. "It's private, Pete."

"Then what the hell is the point of having friends?"

"I keep telling you, it's none of your business. It's between me and God."

Pete threw up his hands in desperation, like a frustrated person giving up, walked a handful of steps away from Dave, then stormed back. "You know what the problem is?"

"I'm sure you'll tell me."

"Maybe Lucy was right. You never reveal the real you, Dave. You never let anyone in. Everything is within your control. But it's bullshit. I see the real Dave every now and then, the passionate one."

Dave looked at Pete askance, his jaw firm and challenging.

"Yeah, that's right, Dave. You're not fooling me. I see through the façade every once in a while. It comes out. That's when I see the real you, and I'm tired of the phony Dave."

"You think I'm a phony?"

"Not all the time, but enough of it. I just wish you'd be more genuine with me. Do you think maybe you aren't genuine with God, either?"

Dave pressed in toward Pete. "Don't stand there and lecture me about the way I live my life, and certainly not about God. You don't know anything about either of them!"

"I know what I see."

"You don't know shit from Shinola! What do you know about life? What do you know about suffering? You didn't grow up trying to survive in the backwaters of Colorado with a dad you were afraid of, a dad who crushed every wild dream you ever had and never, *ever* showed any love or compassion. It was always, 'Do this, don't do that.' And if it wasn't done right, then you did it until it *was* done right. There were no excuses. And there certainly wasn't any of this crap about being real or genuine or whatever you want to call it. My mom died when I was four, so it was just me and the old man! It was survival. And I didn't have a silver spoon in my mouth, unlike you!"

"That stuff is empty, Dave. If—"

"At least you got to find that out!"

Pete waited a moment for a deuce and a half to grind its way past. The truck and a gust of warm wind kicked up the dust. Pete licked his lips, spat, and pointed his empty Coke bottle at Dave's chin.

"Rich people suffer, too, but in other ways."

"What could be worse than wondering whether or not you're gonna starve to death?"

Pete tried to look Dave in the eye, but couldn't. He closed his eyes, the image of his own father filling his head. "Wondering whether or not you matter to your dad."

Dave's eyes narrowed in the lingering dust from the passing truck, and he breathed harder as the conversation grew more tense.

"It's not the same, Pete!" Dave regained some of his composure. "Look, let's just focus on doing our duty. Life is hard enough as it is. Who the hell has time for all that psychological mumbo jumbo?"

"Damn it, Dave, that 'mumbo jumbo' you dismiss is probably what Lucy was talking about back in the hospital, when she told you she wanted your heart."

Dave's eyes widened, and he caught Pete with a hard right uppercut to his chin. Pete's legs buckled, and he collapsed in the dust, the ground smacking him in the head. Dave stomped off down the road, then disappeared around the corner of a row of barracks.

15 - EXPOSURE

Thinking about that day in Texas decades earlier, Pete could almost feel Dave's punch again. A small snowball hit him in the chest, disrupting his thoughts. He looked at Travis with mild shock.

"Pete, I was trying to tell you something. But you seemed like you were in another world."

"What were you saying?"

"That I'm not surprised Dave hit you. No offense."

"None taken. Why aren't you surprised?"

Travis was about to speak when a spasm of pain shot through his legs and he let out a deep groan. Then he regained his composure.

"My dad always told me that you never insult someone's mother. Lucy wasn't Dave's mother, but I figure mentioning someone's wife is a big no-no too."

"You're right, son. That's a pretty wise observation for someone so young."

Travis flashed a weak smile. "Thanks," he said softly.

Pete stared at Travis for a while, trying to sort through something his gut told him might be true. "You're not used to compliments, are you?"

The young snowboarder shook his head no before turning away and fumbling with a zipper on his jacket.

"You don't have to be ashamed, Travis. I knew that feeling, too, when I was your age. I'm sorry you've had to experience that. You deserve better."

A slight nod left Pete wondering if it was a dismissive gesture.

"I know you attend CU, Travis, but where are you from?"

"Ripon, California. It's a little town about an hour and a half east of San Francisco and a little over an hour south of Sacramento. Pretty boring."

"I'm guessing you chose CU for the snowboarding."

Travis let out a knowing laugh, and Pete was glad for the reprieve from their circumstances. It was like a small slice of normalcy.

"Yeah, Pete, I did. It's a common reason. Was it the same in your day?"

"No, it wasn't. You have to remember that skiing was still in its infancy in those days. And Colorado was considered a backwater part of the country. People didn't really know about it. I chose CU because it was Colorado's main university and because of the beauty of the campus. The outdoor activity was a given. So tell me, what does your dad do?"

"He's a water rights attorney. In California that's a pretty lucrative area to specialize in. He's very good at what he does. He's always working."

Pete sensed the sadness in Travis's voice. "Would you ever want to practice law?"

"Hell no!" came the immediate reply.

Pete chuckled. "Wow, you didn't have to think about that one, did you? What's wrong with being an attorney?"

"Is that what you are, Pete?" Travis's tone seemed to hope desperately that Pete wasn't.

A tender, merciful smile crossed Pete's lips. "No, son, I'm not."

Then Travis's face clouded over as he chose his words, like finding the right stones to walk across a swift creek. He scraped some of the snow off the floor of the shelter as he talked. "My dad has given us a really nice life. Really nice. But, well, it just seems like his family has had to pay a big price for it. He's never around. My mom has been lonely for years. She plays tennis and golf at our country club, and she has a lot of lady friends. But I think she'd trade it all in just to have her husband be around. I feel badly for her."

"What about you, Travis? What has life been like for you?"

"I dunno. The same, I guess. There were a lot of important things that happened in my life, and only my mom was present. I made the winning catch in our fourth grade baseball championship. And in eighth grade I won the trophy for most valuable defensive player on our football team. My dad wasn't at the awards ceremony. He and my mom were in Barbados," Travis said, the disgust in his voice thick.

Pete was about to speak, then Travis continued. "Football was my favorite sport. Gosh, I loved it. I played in high school, but my junior year I twisted my ankle pretty badly. I couldn't even practice. I didn't tell my dad about any of it. I was really discouraged and hopeless, so I quit. My dad was really pissed about it. He wouldn't speak to me for days. But, man, if he cared so much about me playing football, why wasn't he at the awards banquet when I was in eighth grade?"

Travis used his gloves to wipe away the tears that had formed in his eyes. He pounded a fist into the snow. Pete said nothing. A few minutes went by. Suddenly Travis said softly, "I would have rather been raised on linoleum in a house where I mattered to my dad than on carpeting in a house where I'm invisible to him."

The shame Pete struggled with, which was always lingering just beneath the surface, raised its head again. *Am I like Travis's dad?* he wondered. *Do I put my "agenda" too often ahead of everyone else's? Your wife might say so, Pete. Maybe your children too. But they know I love them. Of this I'm certain. Yet there are times . . .*

Images of his wife and children flashed through his mind. "You know, Travis, the thing about men is that we want to know we're adequate. We want to know that we have what it takes. It's just that, well, sometimes we get sidetracked in trying to accomplish something in life. So we forget what really matters."

"But that doesn't excuse my dad, Pete. He's caused a hell of a lot of hurt!"

When he was younger, Pete would've felt defensive about Travis's comments. But with age he had learned humility.

Looking at Travis, he said tenderly, "You're right, son. It doesn't excuse his actions. I was merely trying to explain them. Your hurt is real. And hopefully, someday, your dad will understand this. But I have to believe he truly loves you. It took me years, long after my parents were dead, to understand that they truly loved me. They just didn't love me in the way I wanted them to."

"What changed, Pete? What made you realize that they loved you?"

A gust of wind kicked up, scattering snow above their shelter. The images of Pete's parents appeared before him, feeling as real as if they were still alive and the decades hadn't diminished them. Tears welled up in his eyes. A sad but gracious smile formed on his face. "I hated them for a long time. A long time. But I realized that . . ." Pete turned his gaze from Travis for a moment, then looked him in the eye. "I realized they were only human. And that I couldn't demand from them what maybe they were unable to give."

Suddenly feeling uncomfortable with being so vulnerable, Pete adopted a more professorial tone. "You know, as I said, I wanted them to love me a certain way, but they just couldn't." Then he regretted it and scolded himself for sharing.

16 - GOING WHERE THE HOT STUFF COMES FROM

I really miss Dave, Pete thought. *Maybe I should try to patch things up with him, but hell, he's the one who slugged me. He should apologize to me, not the other way around.*

Pete stared into the lukewarm water in the sink of his barracks, then splashed his face again. He prayed for the first time since he was a boy.

God, I'm not sure where to begin. I haven't talked to You since I was a kid. But I guess You know that. Anyway, we'll be heading across the Atlantic in a few days. We don't know where, and I'm more afraid of dying than I thought I'd be. And I wish Dave and I weren't at odds with each other. I feel alone. So I guess I need You, and I'm not used to feeling this way. Please watch over me and Dave. If You get me through the war, I promise to be more mindful of You. Amen.

Temporarily stationed at Camp Patrick Henry in Virginia, before embarkation, the men of the Tenth were given two days' leave in Washington, DC. Pete and several other men boarded a bus for the short ride to the Capitol. They visited a few monuments, and Pete obliged, but his mind was preoccupied with how he'd perform in combat and with thoughts of Dave. Then the group's sightseeing was cut short when one of the men attempted to urinate in the National

Mall reflecting pool after sipping from a flask for a good part of the day. They hustled off in search of a USO dance and found one downtown.

Pete chatted and danced with a brunette named Dolores to the likes of Glenn Miller, Tommy Dorsey, and Artie Shaw. But his heart wasn't in it. Thirsty, he took a break and went to get a Coke. Dizzy, he made his way outside, then promptly vomited in nearby bushes. A soldier passing by came to his aid, helping hold him up.

"Too much to drink tonight, eh, buddy?"

Pete flashed a weak smile and thanked him for his help. He wandered around in the brisk winter night for an hour or so. Then he managed to locate the correct bus back to camp.

On December 11, 1944, Pete, Dave, and the rest of the Eighty-Sixth boarded the USS *Argentina* for a rather slow crossing of the Atlantic, with an escort of destroyers. None of the men knew where in Europe they were headed, and many eased the tension as best they could, lounging, gambling, or smoking. Several days later, as the *Argentina* neared the Strait of Gibraltar, the men of the Eighty-Sixth were finally told where they were headed for combat: Italy.

Pete and Dave had not spoken to each other since their fight at Camp Swift. Pete was up on the rolling deck of the *Argentina* in the dark. He looked at the stars and held an unlit cigarette in his hand, trying to decide whether or not to take up smoking. He thought about everything: what his family was doing, whether or not he was afraid to die and how it might happen, whether or not the German troops in Italy would be tough, and what the terrain would be like. But mostly he thought about Dave. He threw his unused cigarette over the side.

Orion twinkled, and in the inky void of the Atlantic the spray kicked up by the bow of the ship mixed with the constant, icy wind. Pete turned to head below deck when he bumped into a fellow soldier. It was Dave.

"Dave! Dang, sorry about that."

Both men shared an awkward laugh.

"What the hell are you doing up here in this godforsaken wind?" Dave asked.

"Same as you, too nervous, need to clear my head."

"Too much cigarette smoke as well."

Another somewhat awkward laugh.

"I've been looking for you," Dave said. "I wanted to tell you I'm sorry for slugging you back in Texas. I was outta line."

Pete made light of it as best he could. "It's okay. I guess I deserved it for treading on the holy ground of a husband and wife. I never knew you could throw such a mean punch," Pete said, rubbing his chin.

Dave waved off the last comment. "My dad taught me some rudimentary boxing when I was in junior high school. I was having trouble with a bully. Anyway, the wound of Lucy's death was pretty raw, and you just happened to pour salt in it. But I know you didn't mean anything by it."

They shook hands and headed below deck.

On December 23, 1944, the *Argentina* glided into the Bay of Naples on the western coast of Italy, 125 miles south of Rome. Pete was unprepared for what he saw. It was a contrast of war and peace. He stood on the deck of the ship, shoulder to shoulder with hundreds of other soldiers. The serene, jade-green water of the harbor was scarred by wrecked, bombed-out hulks of ships that had met their end and whose forms lay frozen in time, half in the water and half out.

The *Argentina* pulled up to the dock. Pete gathered his canvas duffel bag, slung it over his shoulder with a quick hoist, and headed toward the gang plank. Walking slowly, staring ahead, he shuffled down to the dock with the rest of the Eighty-Sixth.

Naples looked as though it had been caught between the hammer blows of two mighty gods clashing with one another in a fight to the death. Allied and German bombers had laid waste to everything. It seemed as though there was not one intact building standing. Every store, apartment, and building was either a pile of rubble, partially collapsed with the roof caved in, or standing empty with the windows shattered. There were hundreds of shrapnel and bullet scars in the dull, dingy concrete.

Something caught Pete's eye near a shattered storefront. Forlorn and laden with his equipment, he walked toward it. It was a child's toy boat that was squashed flat, left in dozens of pieces. Pete put his bag down and picked up a piece of the wooden toy, one that still had some paint on it. He examined it. In his mind's eye he saw its former glory: intricate, bright, lacquered, and ready for its role in life.

Tugging on his sleeves, a handful of children interrupted Pete's thoughts. They were dirty, and dressed in torn, shredded, colorless clothes. In broken English they begged Pete for chocolate, gum, or any type of food he might have. He quickly searched through his bag and gave them what he had, even his C-rations. This attracted even more children. Pete threw his bag back over his shoulder, pushed his way through the crowd of children, found Lieutenant Loose, and, along with Dave, gathered at the rally point for his platoon. Loose informed them they'd be in Naples a short while, until the Eighty-Fifth and Eighty-Seventh regiments joined them just after the New Year.

On Christmas Pete enjoyed a hot meal of turkey with gravy, instant mashed potatoes, something that might have been stuffing, a dollop of cranberry sauce, and an orange-colored wedge that resembled pumpkin pie. That night Pete lay in his tent with a fellow soldier he didn't know, annoyed that the stranger didn't know when to stop talking and that he made sucking sounds as he smoked his Lucky Strikes.

Pete was surprised he'd gotten a letter from his sister. He read it as he lay in bed that night:

Hi Petey! (I know you wish I'd stop calling you this)

I hope you're doing well. I don't know where this letter will find you. Everyone asks about you all the time. Father always says that he's proud of you and pretends to look forward to you coming home and joining him in the business when the war is over. Ha!

Mother isn't well. The doctors have cooked up some phony

diagnosis I'm sure Father foisted upon them. We all know it's her drinking, but nobody states the obvious.

The weather is as you can imagine it for this time of year in Cleveland—cold, gray, and dreary. I miss seeing you for so many years now. Is it strange to hear from me? Try to write back if you can. Come home alive in '45!

—Betty

Pete folded the letter and tucked it inside the breast pocket of his shirt.

His tent mate babbled about something, then said, "Letter from a girl?"

"Actually, yeah, it is."

"Someone you love?"

"Of course."

"Is she pretty?"

"It's my sister."

"But is she pretty?"

"I don't know, buddy, it's my sister, so just watch what you say." Then Pete looked at the fellow soldier and added, "Yeah, I guess you'd say she's very attractive. She's had boyfriends for years. Would you like her number so you can ask her for a date?"

The other man laughed, boisterous but forced, in a nervous sort of way, then started talking again. Pete fiddled with his bayonet, then attempted to check his M1 rifle, but the light from the candle was too dim.

Pete threw on his pac boots. The Tenth's mountaineering gear, including the hobnailed boots, had been left stateside, so he had no other choice for footwear. He walked outside into the brisk, overcast Italian night. The winter rains had come, and a drizzle fell across him, dampening his spirits as it dampened his clothes. He shivered as he walked past rows of tents. Cigarette smoke mingled with the scent of the wet earth. He managed to find Dave, and together they walked about. Pete thought of the giant Christmas party he was sure his parents were having at their house. Martinis and hors d'oeuvres, champagne and wine, ham, Christmas cake, cognac and brandy, a good cigar, and beautiful ladies powdered and sequined. He chased the thoughts from his mind. He and Dave found the motor pool, and some soldiers huddled near the back end of a deuce and a half. A pungent cloud of cigarette smoke fought the rain for supremacy. Pete and Dave joined the miserable fraternity, and Pete bummed a cigarette off a corporal.

By the first week of January 1945, the Eighty-Fifth and Eighty-Seventh Mountain Infantry Regiments of the Tenth Mountain Division had joined the Eighty-Sixth in Naples. The division hopped on troop transports and sailed up the west coast of Italy to Livorno. The twelve-hour trip was made under the cover of darkness.

Pete and Dave stood on the deck that night, leaning against the steel superstructure. Its cold, freshly painted wall robbed Pets's soul of any desire for adventure, challenge, or esprit de corps.

"We're just 'spear points,' Dave. That's all we are. 'Just get the dirty job done, boys! Win the damn war, and let us get back to our holidays!'"

"Warfare has always been this way, Pete. It's just the way it is."

Pete had been below deck earlier. He'd played some poker, won a few hands, and drunk from his steel flask the harsh grappa he'd scrounged in Naples. It burned on the way down and in his gut. He chomped on a cigar given to him by Sergeant Kirchoff, who'd said some boisterous things about old men and boys in the German army and the effectiveness of the Tenth, and especially the Eighty-Sixth.

The dark shapes of the Italian countryside drifted mutely by, with port and starboard lights here and there and the Tyrrhenian Sea black and calm. Pete chewed on the mashed-up, moist butt of his cigar, then worked hard to eke out a few remaining puffs of rancid smoke. He swigged again from his flask and emptied it. He suddenly had a vision of his life like a parabola that arced through the starry sky above the ship. He saw the coming action as one small point on the arc of his life, like a tiny, distant, blue star. He wondered if he was afraid of combat. He wasn't sure. But he was indeed afraid of something. He just didn't know what. He shivered, and he and Dave went back inside.

The Tenth disembarked in Livorno and boarded a train to Pisa, just over ten miles to the north and east. Pete and Dave lumbered onto the train with the rest of his comrades. Rifles and machine guns, slung on shoulders, clanged. Packs shifted and bounced around, bayonets and entrenching shovels jangled, helmet chin straps swayed, and boots clomped down the passageways. Pete wedged himself in. The air inside the train smelled of sweat, the earth, tobacco, soap, coffee, and alcohol on the breath.

Pete wanted to look up and gaze at the faces of his brother soldiers, but he didn't. He stared at the floor instead and saw boots, pair upon pair. He felt hollow, cold, and cowardly. The train slowed, and his head jerked up, catching the nervous glances of his comrades. This was it. They were close to the Winter Line now. Occupied Italy lay beyond, where the Germans protected the breadbasket of northern Italy, the Po River Valley.

Pete walked off the train with everyone else as quietly as he could. It was dark, and the cold sank into his bones. Company A gathered around Captain Jay, their commander. Pete shivered and pressed in toward Jay. The company was packed close. The warmth felt good.

Captain Jay informed them they'd be moving on up to their staging area for an assault on a mountain called Belvedere. Traveling by day was safe, since the U.S. Army Air Corps controlled the skies. They would go by truck, then walk up to the line. They would encamp discreetly in the villages near Belvedere. Once they were there, they would move only at night to avoid detection by the Germans, who occupied the high ground of Mount Belvedere and the surrounding hills. Further orders would be delivered once the division was in place.

The commanding officer, General George Hays, wanted his most skilled soldiers in the Eighty-Sixth up on the line as quickly as possible, so he had them loaded aboard trucks. The rest of the regiment would follow on foot. The selected men of the Eighty-Sixth were ordered to find an assault route up a three-and-a-half-mile-long mountain dubbed Riva Ridge by the Americans. The ridge was being used by the Germans as an observation post to direct artillery fire from nearby Mount Belvedere down toward the multinational U.S. Fifth Army in the valley below.

The strong, rough hand of a fellow soldier helped Pete into the back of a deuce and a half. The truck filled up, Dave among them. The truck's driver engaged the gears, and they headed out with a jerk. The truck's covered bed was like a cave, and Pete felt glum and isolated. Little amber dots glowed and faded as men lit cigarettes, puffed, and exhaled. Pete reached inside his coat and pulled out his flask. He shook it—empty.

The big truck ground slowly through the Italian landscape. There were four other trucks in the convoy. They wound toward the front line stopping again and again, for who knew what, then jerked forward, bouncing and jolting along. Pete tried to sleep. He dozed off when the convoy stopped, but the deteriorated condition of the road made prolonged rest impossible. They drove through the day. Pete was tired but also edgy, mostly from the unknown situation ahead. They stopped during dusk and lay down in a small field with only their blankets. Tents and sleeping bags were forbidden this close to the front line.

Pete lay next to Dave. It was cold, but he wasn't prepared for the deeper chill that clung to the ground. He exchanged a few gripes with the men nearby about the day's trip, then bedded down. But he couldn't get warm and was in and out of a stupor of half-sleep.

He awoke to the sound of an airplane flying low overhead. Its throaty, powerful engine punched its way over the foothills of the Apennines. Startled at first, Pete thought maybe it was a German Messerschmitt preparing to strafe them where they lay. Then he caught his bearings as the airplane faded away.

A nearby voice said, "P38."

"What?" Pete said.

"P38. One of ours. That was a P38 Lightning that just flew by."

"How can you tell?"

"The sound of twin engines moving very fast. Nothing else sounds so loud yet moves so quickly, brother."

Pete felt stupid and incompetent, as though this was common knowledge he should've known.

The new day was clear, and hoarfrost covered everything. Men were walking around. Pete threw off his heavy blanket, which was damp on its surface, and sat up, trying to work out the stiffness that reminded him of his hard night's sleep. Men lit their field stoves, boiled water, and wolfed down K-rations. The smell of coffee wafted through the air, and Pete decided he'd make some as well.

An hour later he, Dave, and the rest of his brothers from the Eighty-Sixth crammed back into a heavy truck and slowly rumbled north. Pete held his M1 between his legs, resting the butt on the floor of the truck. He stared out from the low brim of his steel helmet, searching the dark hollows of each face.

I wonder how each of you will perform under fire, Pete wondered. *Will I die, and if so, how? A Nazi bullet? A grenade? I hope I don't fall to my death. That would be too ironic, a soldier trained to scale mountains dying because he couldn't.*

It was another slow passage, and the men in Pete's truck swayed in unison, rocking and bouncing, smoking, saying nothing. They rolled on, stopping and starting, holding up, being waved through. It was balmy for a winter day. Pete dozed off again, and dreamt.

He was a boy again, visiting Niagara Falls with his family. He rounded a corner, and there was Dave, also a boy, who said, "Come on, Pete, I'll show you how to get across!"

Pete followed Dave. They were in the city one moment, then running through woods the next. They came to a riverbank upstream from the falls. There was a thick rope stretched across the river. Dave walked out on it, holding a long pole in his hands for balance. He got to the middle, did a little Irish jig, looked over his shoulder and smiled at Pete, then walked the rest of the way across.

When he got to the far bank, he shouted back, "Now you do it, Pete!"

Pete had a long pole in his hands as well. He decided he would vault the river instead. He backed up, ran hard, leaped from the bank and thrust the pole into the middle of the swift current.

Dave shouted, "No, Pete, you'll never make it! You must follow me!"

Pete arced over the river and held the pole tight, but it fell short. He plunged into the river, sank down, and felt himself drowning. His lungs hurt and yearned for air. His head throbbed, and he looked up at the distant surface, knowing he couldn't make it. Then he heard his father talking to his mother and saw them, up through the water, standing on the bank.

His father said, "He isn't going to make it, dear. Let's go."

They turned and left. But suddenly Dave was next to Pete, there under the water. Dave had wings of wax. They reminded Pete of Icarus. Dave held out his hand. There was a hunk of bread in his palm. He said, "Take this, Pete, and you'll live." Pete chewed and swallowed the bread, and he and Dave shot out of the water like cannon balls. They were flying through the air now. Pete had grown wings too!

They flew far above the Earth, so high that it grew distant. They touched down on the surface of the Moon. Everything was dry and white. Pete and Dave stared at the Earth.

"Now do you see, Pete?"

The truck jolted, and Pete woke with a start. *Geez, that was a weird dream. I understand my parents abandoning me, but what was going on with the bread and the Moon?*

He couldn't get the image of the bread out of his mind. Then he remembered. *The bread represents God! Maybe I learned something from Sunday School after all. Didn't Jesus talk about Himself as bread? What did He call Himself? The Bread of Life, right? I think that's right. So I'm supposed to turn to God to keep from dying? Is that it, God?*

"If you really want to live, yes."

Pete was certain one of the other soldiers said it. He glanced around. Nothing but blank stares and heads hung among the men, except for Dave, who gave him a concerned look. The more he thought about the words and whether it was indeed God speaking to him, the more his fear left him. He didn't feel so alone anymore. He didn't know what would happen in the coming battle, but something inside him trusted that everything would be okay. *Is this what faith truly is?* he wondered.

By the end of the day the convoy was slowing, stopping, and starting again more frequently. They were close to the staging area now. The inside of Pete's mouth was like cotton. He snuck a quick sip from his flask and chased it with water from his canteen. The truck slowed again, then stopped. The driver and another soldier appeared at the back and unhinged the tailgate. Pete jumped down with the rest of the men. The sun had set, and the sky was violet. Pete wondered what the order would be. Just then a jeep crept up, stopped, and Captain Jay stood up on the passenger seat, holding onto the windshield. He had the men of the convoy gather around himself. He gave the order to move out quietly into the village of Vidiciatico, which was just ahead, and to seek lodging among the locals, who were awaiting the arrival of the Americans.

Pete, along with Dave and the rest of the men from his truck, approached what appeared to be a small farm or orchard. A small, squat sergeant knocked on the door, while a dark-haired private stood beside him. A middle-aged couple answered, and the dark-haired soldier interpreted for the sergeant. The noncommissioned officer split the small platoon in two; half would stay in the house, half would stay in the barn. Pete was standing near the front of the group and was selected to stay in the house.

He trudged inside with the sergeant, the interpreter, Dave, and two other men. It was warm, almost hot. A fire burned in a black stove, and a large pot sat on top of it, steam curling up. The scent of baking bread graced the air. Pete's mouth watered, and he wiped saliva from the crease of his lips.

The woman directed him and the rest of the soldiers to an area on a wooden floor toward the back of the small house. They followed the farmer's wife, the rough boards creaking under their slow, measured steps. They dropped their duffels. The woman mimicked an eating motion with her hands, and they understood. Each man grabbed his mess tin. Then she herded them back toward the simple, warm kitchen where she ladled steaming soup into each man's canteen cup and handed each of them a hunk of warm bread. Pete devoured half of the bread before he sat down cross-legged on the floor near the stove. He dunked the rest of his bread in the reddish soup and crammed it in his mouth. He held the steaming cup near his face and ate as fast as he could without burning his tongue. When he got up, the farmer's wife was still at the stove; she filled his cup again and gave him some more bread. Again he sat down and ate everything within minutes. He licked his spoon clean, walked to the back of the house, and placed his mess kit near his duffel.

He glanced over his shoulder, then pulled out his bottle of grappa and filled his canteen cup half-full. He shoved the bottle back in his duffel between some extra clothes. Then he took his filled-up flask from his jacket and hid it in one of the pockets of his fatigue pants and walked back toward the kitchen. He held his cup with both hands, sipping.

A while later the farmer came in through the back door. He clutched three bottles of wine and walked to the small kitchen table. He set the bottles down loudly and babbled on in Italian. The sergeant asked for an interpretation, and the dark-haired soldier said the farmer wanted them to drink some wine with him. Pete walked to the table and sat down quickly, his cup at the ready. The farmer opened all three bottles, each of a different shape. He chose one and filled Pete's canteen cup almost to the top. The interpreter and the sergeant joined him at the table, as did one of the other three men. Of the remaining two soldiers, one was in the back trying to sleep and the other was engrossed in smoking a cigarette and writing a letter. The farmer filled each man's cup as well as his own.

Then the farmer stood up, raised his cup, and said in a thick accent, "God bless America. *Salute.*"

The rest of the men at the table echoed his Italian blessing in unison and drank. Within an hour most of the wine was gone. The farmer left and came back with three more bottles. Pete savored the robust red wine, listening to the dark-haired soldier interpret the farmer's words.

He talked about how he hated Mussolini and his Blackshirts,

almost as much as he hated the Germans. He said he had lied about his age during the First World War in order to join a unit of the Alpini, the rugged Italian mountain troops. He wasn't even seventeen years old when he helped fight the Austrians to a standstill in the bitter climate of the Italian Alps, above the northern lake region of Italy. The dark-haired soldier explained to him the nature and purpose of the Tenth Mountain Division, but was careful not to reveal too much. The farmer grew animated.

"*Momento*," he said, and disappeared out the back door of the house.

He came back a few minutes later with his arms full of equipment. He dumped it on the kitchen table, knocking over one of the bottles of wine. It was climbing gear. He explained that it was his equipment from thirty years earlier, when he was part of the Alpini. There was a long, wooden ice axe with the varnish long gone, banged-up pitons that were now rusted, a coiled, frayed, worn rope, and the crown jewel of the collection: fine, handmade, Italian leather climbing boots that were still in good condition. It was obvious Nicholas the farmer was proud of his boots and had worked to keep the leather soft and dark, almost like new.

Pete grabbed the boots, examining the leather. It was supple and still beautiful. Then he turned the boots upside down and inspected the hobnails in the toes and on the edges and was surprised to find them in good condition too. They were still firm in the sole. Since he and Nicholas were of about the same height, he took a chance and hurriedly tried the boots on. They fit perfectly.

To Pete's shock and delight, the farmer offered him the boots. Pete initially declined the offer out of politeness. When the farmer persisted, Pete gave in. Somewhat overcome by the moment and too much wine, Pete's eyes welled up. The farmer was emotional as well, hugging Pete's stiff body and kissing him on each cheek.

These are good omens. If only I can wear these things without getting caught and having to turn them in, I'll be doing swell!

Over the month of January, they waited for the arrival of the rest of the Eighty-Sixth regiment, along with the Eighty-Fifth and the Eighty-Seventh. Pete, Dave, and a few other men from his company,

along with a larger number of men from another company, partici-
pated in numerous night patrols across the Dardagna River, along the
base of Riva Ridge. They were trying to find possible routes of ascent
in preparation for their coming assault on the German troops, who
occupied the top of the ridge. They had been ordered to do so by
General Hays.

One night toward the end of January, Pete headed out on a reconnaissance patrol along with three other men from his company, though
Dave was not one of them. The man leading the patrol was an athletic-
looking sergeant named Lamb.

Pete had regained much of the strength he'd lost. He'd lost some of
his fitness from the inactivity of being transported from Camp Swift to
Virginia, then across the Atlantic, the waiting in Naples, and then
moving to Livorno and Pisa. His body always responded quickly to
physical activity, and he built muscle easily on his slightly compact,
athletic frame.

Pete and the other men traveled along the river, moving from
south to north. The ground was illuminated by an old, thin, crusty
layer of snow that did its best to avoid melting entirely. The path by
the river twisted this way and that. It was well-worn, long devoid of
snow and only muddy now. The river was low, but still loud enough to
conceal most sounds nearby. It babbled steadily. Riva Ridge loomed to
the left, nearly five thousand feet up, its black mass filling the horizon.
They were traveling to its northern tip, as they had done three nights
earlier, leaving shortly after dark and a hot meal.

Pete angled his watch toward the waxing half-moon to get a better
view. It was past eight o'clock now. His new climbing boots conformed
to his feet and were as comfortable as he'd hoped.

*God bless these Italians! Darn if they don't know how to make the best
shoes in the world.*

The small patrol reached the turnoff for the Campiano and
headed north and west. They came to the edge of the woods that
lined the Dardagna River, and crouched in a huddle, waiting. They
had to cross a clearing that ran for several hundred meters and was
slightly uphill. The field glowed in the moonlight, its old snow still
glistening.

Perfect! Just what we need—a white backdrop to make it easier for the Krauts to pick us off, Pete thought.

Sergeant Lamb whispered, "Okay guys, I'll go first. We'll leapfrog across this piece of crap as quick and quiet as we can. The last man will tap me on the shoulder as he runs by. Here we go."

Lamb held his carbine with one hand and then, hunching down, sprinted over the snow as best he could. Pete held his M1 tight in both hands and adjusted his climbing rope, draped over his shoulder like a bandolier strap. He was next. He headed out. The crunch of the snow filled his ears.

Shit! The Krauts are probably lining up a shot on me right now!

He kept moving, passing Sergeant Lamb, who squatted motionless on the snow. Pete's mouth was like cotton, and his lips were dry. His heart pounded like drums in his head, and he squeezed the stock of his M1. His rope weighed him down and swayed on his body clumsily. He tried to tell himself to stop breathing so loudly. He decided he'd gone far enough and crouched in the snow. He stared at the dark, safe woods ahead.

"Come on, you bastards, hurry up," he whispered to himself.

One man passed him, crunching as he went by. He waited for a rifle shot he was certain was going to come from somewhere up above. Nothing happened. Another man passed him now. Pete waited. Next came Sergeant Lamb, who tapped Pete's shoulder. The sergeant was still moving up ahead when Pete decided he could wait no longer and started off again. He shot past Street, a fellow private, who was down on one knee, sucking in air. The woods were close now. Pete almost kept going, but stopped and knelt again in the snow as he'd been instructed, maintaining his discipline. He crouched again as low as he could. The crunch of the steps of the man approaching behind him grew louder.

Suddenly a rifle shot ripped the stillness apart. Pete dove for the ground, pressing into the hard, crusty snow. Breathing hard, another soldier plopped next to Pete with a thud. The sergeant and the fourth soldier bolted past.

"Make for the woods!" Lamb commanded in a harsh whisper.

Pete was up and flying across the clearing.

Another shot rang out. He thought he saw a cloud of snow kick up to his left, but was too frightened to look. Ragged breaths filling his ears, he raced, desperate for the dark haven. Unable to see and with the fourth man right behind, Pete crashed into the man ahead of him.

"Take it easy," Street growled. "You're gonna wake up the whole stinkin' German army!"

"Sorry, buddy," Pete said.

"Everybody just relax," Lamb commanded. He gasped a few times, still trying to catch his breath.

"The Krauts know we're here, but it's a big ridge, so we should be fine. The closer in we get, the more defilade we have. Be silent and don't make mistakes, 'cause we can either do this right or do it twice. Let's go."

There was more snow here. They followed their path from two nights before. Twisted chestnut trees mottled the hillside, their arms extended as if ready to snag the invaders in the Moon's silver light. The trail wound higher, angling toward the shoulder of the Pizzo di Campiano. The trees thinned out and were smaller. Pete estimated they were a few thousand feet below the summit. It was almost 10:30 p.m.

Then the trail grew even steeper. Blue Spruce and Austrian Pine sat silently in the thinner snow. But there were patches of ice. Each man slung his rifle over his shoulder and used both hands to hoist up, bound over rocks, and grab tree roots.

This isn't too technical, Pete mused. *We should be able to get a lot of men up this pretty quickly.*

Pete glanced at his watch. It was almost midnight now. He sweated heavily. The group set a pattern of climbing for ten minutes, resting for one minute, climbing for another ten, so Pete was glad they'd been ordered to climb with as little gear as possible, in order to move silently. The trail was now devoid of trees or any other protection.

We're really exposed here! No trees, the Moon is out, and we're making noise. I'm sure we've alerted the Krauts by now. We're probably heading into a trap.

Pete felt certain they were about 1,000 to 1,500 feet below the summit. Then they came to the first truly technical section of the route. It looked to be fifty to sixty feet high. It wasn't completely vertical, but it had enough of a pitch that the group made the decision to fix a rope.

Sergeant Lamb chose himself to make the climb, with Pete on belay. The other two men stood lookout. The trail was fairly narrow here, perhaps three feet wide, and the side of it dropped steeply away into black trees far below. It was almost vertical and similar to the rock face they were about to climb.

For this technical section they used rope belonging to another soldier instead of Pete's. Lamb scanned the dark, knobby rock looking for holds and making note of icy patches; there were plenty of each. He slung his rifle across his back.

Pete fed the rope as Lamb climbed—five feet, ten feet. Lamb paused, held onto the rock, and reached for a piton and his rock hammer. The piton wedged into the rock. Then the sergeant put a snap ring in place, clipped in the rope, and moved higher. Four more times he did this as Pete played out the rope.

Then Lamb disappeared over the lip at the top of the wall. Pete fed him more line. A few minutes later Lamb was back at the top of the wall. In a loud whisper he called for the rest of the group to climb up and use the same rope. Pete held on to the rope while his two other comrades climbed up. Then he did the same. The rope he carried with him chafed his neck and face and made the going clumsy. It was heavy too. Pete finally reached the top, winded. He had to rest briefly and was doubled over. But Lamb didn't wait long and kept the group moving. Pete pressed after them and finally caught his breath as they moved away from the rock wall. The trail's grade slackened for a few hundred meters.

Past one a.m. the patrol came to another technical section. It appeared to be the final one, as the terrain above them was more rounded and tapered off, giving way to the starry sky. It was a vertical rock face and looked to be about twenty feet high or so. Pete and the sergeant ran their hands over the rock, noting the thin coating of ice. Pete pulled off his coil of rope.

"Looks like you're up, McGregor," Lamb said quietly. "Ready?"

"Ready as I'm ever gonna be, Sarge," Pete whispered. "Just give me a minute to get my gear ready."

Pete got his hammer, pitons, and snap rings ready so he could reach them quickly and easily.

"On belay?"

"Belay on," Lamb said, just above a whisper.

Pete moved too quickly at first. He was only a few moves up when his foot slipped on a tiny, icy edge. Luckily he had both hands on the rock and caught himself. He was stretched out, his legs dangling. He cursed his haste, slowed down, and tried to see the icy spots in the moonlight, but it was difficult. Almost halfway up he found a narrow crack. He pulled up on the rope, made a loop, clasped it in his teeth, then reached for his hammer and a piton. He tapped it in, placed the snap ring, clipped the rope in, and kept going. He was eager and felt good and strong. Near the top he placed another piton and clipped the rope in again. Now all he had to do was clear the top edge and look for a rock or root with which to anchor the rope.

Pete lunged over the top and searched for something to anchor his rope. He looked around for a few seconds, then found a solid root and tied off his rope. He turned back toward the edge of the rock wall. Suddenly he spotted a dark figure to his right moving toward him. He dropped to the ground as quickly and quietly as he could.

Shit! I'm dead. That has to be a Kraut. They're the only ones up here. I'll never be able to unsling my rifle before he shoots me. Damn it!

Crunching footsteps grated on the rock, getting closer.

That guy is moving really slow. Has he seen me?

Pete's face was pressed into the ground. But he had to get a look at the figure, to determine what he was up to. Pete felt for his bayonet, which was strapped inside his jacket, and slid it out. Then he slowly lifted his cheek off the ground and turned his head. The familiar shape of the soldier's German helmet caught his attention. But he wasn't looking at Pete. His head was turned sideways. The German gazed downward into the black fold of the valley between the Pizzo di Campiano and Monte Cappel Buso, its neighboring southern peak.

The enemy soldier walked closer, heading straight toward Pete. He was no more than thirty meters away now. Pete readied himself, preparing to pounce. The crunch of the German's boots filled his ears. He thought only of killing the man. If he alerted his comrades, the whole mission could be jeopardized.

If he's part of a patrol, the whole operation will be blown. Damn my luck! Where the hell did this bastard come from?

Just then Pete heard a muffled shout from below. It was Sergeant Lamb, calling Pete's name. Alerted now, the German soldier walked toward the edge of the small cliff, his machine gun at the ready, and peered down. Immediately the German crouched low.

Pete watched and waited, unsure what he should do. The soldier looked down and seemed about to shoot. Then he hesitated. Instead he pulled out a grenade—a German "potato masher." He twisted the top to activate it, and tossed it below. It clanged as it hit the ground below.

Someone shouted, "Grenade!"

The high-pitched concussion rolled through the valley, bounced back, then died away. There were more shouts below, and confusion.

Someone fired back a single, clean rifle shot.

The German pumped out a few rounds from his machine gun. There was no response from below at first.

Another rifle shot.

The German was shooting blind, Pete was convinced, unsure where the Americans were. The men below had protection from the enemy's machine gun, due to the overhanging rock, but not from his grenades. Pete had to make a move.

Bayonet in hand, Pete rose carefully and moved toward the German. The enemy soldier was engrossed in his firefight with the Americans below. He hadn't noticed Pete nor had he seen the rope Pete anchored at the top of the cliff, at least not yet. Pete was twenty meters away now, then fifteen. There were more futile shots and more shouts from below. He was ten meters from his enemy. He had never come in contact with a German soldier before. Pete saw everything clearly: the camouflage smock, the black boots, the gas mask canister, and the rounded canteen.

Pete was five meters from him now when the German reached back for another grenade. He fumbled for it, then looked up and saw

Pete. Each other's eyes widened, and Pete lunged. He hit the German with full force, but the loose footing blunted his attack. Pete held his bayonet in an iron grip, with the blade pointing down, so that he could swing it downward and hack, if need be. He tried to thrust his blade into the German's chest, but the soldier caught Pete's wrist and tumbled backward, with Pete on top of him. They rolled over, and Pete's knuckles crunched into the rocks as the German's helmet fell off. He dropped his bayonet in pain and let out a yelp. The German lay askew on top of Pete. Pete twisted his torso hard and managed to roll the man off him. The German's machine gun clattered against the rocks beneath his body. Pete couldn't shake free of the soldier's grip.

Now angry and frustrated, Pete jerked his arms free, got behind the soldier, and wrapped his arm around the German's neck. The soldier searched for Pete's bayonet, trying to grab it. Pete yelled in desperation and rolled the man over on top of himself, away from the weapon. Pete was beneath him, but his arm was still wrapped around the man's neck like a vice. As the German was twisting free, Pete fumbled, groped, and grabbed the man by the chin and the hair on the back of his head. He twisted his head as hard as he could, snapping his neck. The German's body went limp, and Pete rolled him off.

Pete lay in the cold moonlight, his arm draped across his face. Everything was quiet while he caught his breath and tried to shake off what had just happened, but he knew he must hurry. He sat up. There were sharp whispers below. He looked around nervously, searching for the dead soldier's companions who might be lurking and waiting to attack. But he saw no one.

He walked to the rope anchor and tested the knot he'd made, then called down quietly over the cliff's edge to his comrades, beckoning them up the rope. Then he walked over to the dead soldier. His smooth, well-fed face looked like wax. His blue eyes were open, and his mouth was agape. Pete shivered, but he couldn't look away for a long time, transfixed by what he'd done. He remembered his flask and took a long drink of the grappa inside. He looked again at the German's face. The odor of the man's sweat and shaving soap gently wafted up. Pete frowned, closed his eyes, and swigged hard again. He wiped some excess from the corner of his mouth, then searched the body quickly, shaking as he did so. He told himself it was because of the cold. He found a wallet and a knife and put them inside his jacket. He turned away sharply and walked back to the rope.

Lamb was already at the top of the cliff, watching the progress of the other two soldiers below. As Pete approached, Lamb studied his face.

"You all right, McGregor?"

"I killed him, Sarge. I broke his neck. But shit, I thought he had me. I hope I never have to go through that again."

"I can smell the alcohol on you a mile away. Lay off that stuff, will you? We've got a long trip back."

"The Kraut's over there," Pete said softly, gesturing behind without looking back. "What should we do with the body?"

"We'll have to toss it over the cliff here, then we'll roll it off the trail when we get down below, down into the woods, and cover it with branches. Maybe the Krauts will think he deserted. I don't want them to know, in any way, that we've been up here. If they come snooping around, they may find our rope, and then the whole assault might have to be called off. So drag the body over here."

"Right, Sarge."

Pete trudged back over to the German, avoided his face, grabbed him by the boot, and dragged him over the rocks to the rope anchor. Then he dropped the leg and walked to the other side of the sergeant.

The third soldier in the patrol suddenly appeared, scrambling up over the cliff edge. The body of the dead German caught his attention.

"Holy shit! Was that from you, McGregor?"

Pete looked at him blankly. Then he turned away and walked slowly back to the dead body. He put the man's wallet back where he found it.

"Forgive me, God," he prayed quietly. "I didn't know what else to do. I pray I never have to do that again, and that his body finds its way back to his parents. I'm sure they worry about him and . . ."

He couldn't finish, grief choking his throat.

The third soldier walked over to the German, stared, then turned around and lit a cigarette, cupping the end to conceal the orange glow.

Lamb said to the soldier, "Turn around and keep an eye out for any more Krauts."

The private obeyed, snuffing out his cigarette and desperately scanning the darkness.

The fourth soldier, Street, appeared now over the lip. Like the one before, he saw the dead German and exclaimed, "Holy crap! What happened...?"

"Save it," Lamb said. "We're wasting too much time. Form up, let's go."

The sergeant led the men up a scree field. They had to move slowly to avoid kicking up the loose rocks. Pete had his rifle ready, gripping it tightly. He and the rest of the group were completely exposed; there were no trees or shrubs or boulders for cover. Pete's body ached, and he wanted to stop and drink something, anything. He thought he kept seeing an enemy soldier up ahead and envisioned a bullet with his name on it. They made it through the scree, and the summit seemed close at hand. Sergeant Lamb led them up a shoulder of rock and onto a gentler pitch. Pete imagined being on the Moon. A wind kicked up and sent a shiver through Pete. The sergeant stopped just ahead, motioning Pete and the others to his side. They crouched, huddling in the wind.

Lamb whispered hoarsely, "Okay, men, that's the summit right there," as he pointed with his hand like a karate chop. "That's about a hundred meters. So we hustle our butts up there, take a quick look around, then get the hell off before Jerry knows we paid him a visit. Follow me."

The group hustled up the last section of the climb quickly and easily. Just a few feet below the top, someone kicked a large rock loose. Everyone froze. Pete's jaw clamped tight, and his eyes darted over his shoulder toward a distant patch of low trees and scrub. He was almost certain the Germans were out there in the shadows, marking them and waiting for the right moment. Lamb sprang silently up to the summit. Pete and the others waited, watching him search the darkness. Then he turned back toward them, signaled an about-face, and Pete and the other two soldiers headed back down the mountain.

They got back to the top of the small cliff. Pete passed the dead body, slung his rifle, and grabbed the fixed rope as he was about to repel down.

"McGregor, what are you doing? Roll that body over the side," Lamb said.

Cringing, unable to look at the man he'd killed, Pete did as he was ordered. Seconds later the body hit the ground with a clanking, sickening thud. Pete felt numb. He grabbed the rope and repelled down. The body lurked in his periphery, like some kind of specter waiting to haunt him. He held the rope and fixed his gaze back up the rock wall. Sergeant Lamb came down next. After he was down, Pete heard him rolling the body toward the edge of the path. He didn't look, keeping his gaze on the rope and his comrades as they repelled down. Then he heard the body crashing into the trees below. He fought the urge to bolt from his comrades and run down the way he'd come up. Instead, he stayed where he was until the other two got down safely.

"Can we get the hell down now, Sarge?"

"Move out," the sergeant ordered.

Pete started walking while the words were still on Lamb's lips.

17 - FIGHTING FOR THE HIGH GROUND

At the beginning of February, Pete's platoon commander, Lieutenant James Loose, briefed his men in a small, rundown barn.

"We've got five routes up Riva Ridge now, men. The Krauts are unaware of this, but not for long. So we're gonna assault the summit on the eighteenth, sometime after midnight. But we've got to take the whole ridge in one night."

Men cursed, but not Pete. He and Dave exchanged glances, knowing what the other was thinking. They could take the ridge in one night, but it would be tricky, with hardly any margin for error.

"The main assault will take place at dawn," Loose continued. "But prior to this, Companies A, B, C, and D of the First Battalion, and Company F of the Second Battalion, will scale Riva in the dark, eliminate any German resistance on top, and hold off any counterattacks until reinforcements arrive. Any questions?"

"When can we expect reinforcements?" one soldier asked.

"Two days, or so I'm told."

Two days, Pete thought. *I think we can hold the summit for two days, but beyond that? Hell, I don't want to think about it—cold, hunger, exhaustion...death.* He shivered at the thought of it.

.   .   .

A couple of weeks later, a few days before the attack, Major General Hays bucked convention and personally addressed the men of the Tenth.

"There won't be any artillery or aerial bombardment before you begin the assault. I don't want the element of surprise compromised in any way. You will move on up the mountain in silence. Fix your bayonets, but do not load any ammunition in your rifles. I do not want any premature firing alerting the enemy as to our intentions. We'll only have one good shot at this, men. Never get pinned down. Move forward. There will be no order to turn back. Good luck."

Pete was in the crowd. *Never get pinned down?* he thought. *Easy for you to say, General.* Images of the man he'd killed filled his head.

What will his mother do? She'll only know that he's MIA, probably assume he was KIA. Was that her only child? She never thought he'd end up this way when he was born, did she? No. How old was he? Twenty? Twenty-one? Was he a decent man or a pig?

Hays finished talking, and the men headed over to a field kitchen to have an early, hot meal before dark. Pete and Dave, along with the rest of their company, walked to their duffels and blankets. They'd be traveling light. Lieutenant Loose told them to grab only their weapons and ammunition, along with their canteens and whatever they could scrounge from their K-ration boxes.

Pete clipped on his canteen and stuffed some chocolate bars and crackers inside his jacket. Crouching low, he filled his flask. He only had enough grappa to fill it halfway. Then he slipped it quickly into his coat pocket. He made sure he had his full complement of ammunition, ninety-six rounds, in his bandolier strap. He'd been given a piece of white tape, like everyone else. He was told to place this on the back of his helmet, in order to determine friend from foe in the dark.

Just after 7:00 p.m. Sergeant Lamb kicked Pete, waking him. He got up in a daze and rolled up his blanket.

At 7:30 p.m. the Eighty-Sixth began its silent assault on Riva Ridge. Pete headed up the trail, following the Dardagna, which swept swiftly past in an early purge of winter's shroud.

Pete thought of Dave, who was here somewhere in the dark, anxious, just like himself and everyone else. The German corpse flashed in his mind again, with its lifeless eyes and the mouth open. He shook his head, then picked up his pace.

They exited the woods and moved fast and low, across the open field where Pete had been shot at earlier. Pete's mouth was dry and he breathed hard, but he made it across without incident.

The trail became steeper, snaking up the fold toward the summit of the Campiano. A dense fog rolled in. Pete could barely see beyond the man directly in front of him. Like the others, he grasped at the exposed roots and small trees that dotted the route. He didn't have his rope to weigh him down, but the full ammunition belt made up for it. He breathed harder this time, and the closer he climbed to the place of the fallen German he'd killed, the thicker and colder the fog felt. The platoon's pace was steady now.

They approached the first technical section, climbed it using the rope placed in the rock by Sergeant Lamb, and plodded higher. The trail's incline was at its steepest now. Lieutenant Loose led the charge. Pete was the third man back. The fog was thick. All he could do was follow the man in front of him. They were high now. The ice was more prevalent, and the wind kicked up. Pete was working so hard that the cold, rushing wind was actually a relief. Slowly the fog began to weaken.

The man in front of Pete stopped, along with Lieutenant Loose up ahead. Pete approached.

Loose asked, "Either of you guys know where in the hell we are? How close are we?"

Pete looked at his watch—12:06 a.m., only hours before the main assault would begin.

"From our scout patrols, Lieutenant, I'd say we're close to the last technical section. After that we've got a field of loose rocks, then about four hundred easy meters to the summit. But at that point there won't be any protection from enemy fire."

"Okay, McGregor, you lead us from here."

The hair on the back of Pete's neck stood up, and immediately his palms began sweating. *I'll just bet some Kraut is waiting higher up, itching to send me home in a coffin.*

Pete took the lead, and in minutes the cliff loomed just ahead. The abyss of the dark valley was to his left. He thought he smelled putrid flesh but climbed on, glancing over into the dark fold below. Distracted, he lost his footing and twisted his ankle as he fell, grabbing an exposed root as he began to slide off the path, into the shadowy crease. *No!* his mind screamed, and he imagined the dead man's face staring up at him, awaiting his fall.

Pete knocked down the man directly behind him, who rolled off the trail, tumbled below, and cried out. Loose responded immediately, detailing the next few men in the line to assist Pete and the other fallen soldier. He told Pete to sit and wait for help, who ignored the order and clumsily scrambled up on his good foot. Then he slipped on some ice and fell again. His ankle felt like it was on fire, and he could feel it swelling already. Another soldier grabbed his arm and helped him up.

Son of a bitch! Pete thought. *What the hell is wrong with me? I'm stumbling all over the hillside like a damn drunkard.*

"Just get me to the cliff up there," Pete said, nodding toward the next rock face.

"That's the spirit, McGregor," Loose said. "We need every man on the summit that we can get."

Desperate to minimize his pain and make it to the summit, Pete did his best to stay quiet.

"Let's keep moving. Get him over to the rope," Loose told the man next to Pete. "He can hold it steady and be our anchor. You follow him up the rope and make sure he makes it. You two are the last men up. Got that?"

"Yes, sir," responded both men.

Then Loose turned his attention to the rescue of the man Pete had rolled into and knocked into the ravine. Pete stumbled over to the rock face, with the other man's help, and sat down hard and awkward at the base of the fixed rope.

Suddenly the crunch of boots came toward them. The next soldier in line approached, a shadowed form emerging from the fog. It was David Bates.

Relief washed over Pete. *Thank you, God,* he prayed.

"Glad to see you, Dave."

"What happened to you, buddy?" Dave asked, quickly kneeling beside him.

"I sprained my damn ankle and almost slid off the trail, down the ravine. I need to make it to the top, though."

"I know, Pete. We've come so far." Then Dave's eyes widened. "Why don't I give you one of my morphine vials?"

"Do it," Pete mumbled, as sharp pains shot through his ankle.

Dave injected the morphine into Pete's thigh, then walked to the rope, grabbed it, scanned the little cliff, and gave the rope a jerk. "Who placed the rope? Do we know how strong the anchors are?"

"I placed it, Dave."

"Then I'm sure it's fine."

Despite the pain, Pete felt a deep sense of pride and a depth of love for his friend he didn't know he had.

Dave climbed up the cliff. His rubberized pac boots made the going difficult for him. Pete and the other soldier watched him struggle to find footholds for his ungainly boots and heard him curse the U.S. Army the whole way up. When he was near the crest of the rock wall, Pete felt the rope start to give. The pitons were coming loose! Pete wondered if the anchor up top had somehow come undone. His heart and mind raced, and he didn't know what to do. If the rope was giving way, Dave was too high up to come back down in time. He tried to will Dave to the top of the cliff, biting his tongue.

Near the lip of the wall, Dave placed all his weight on the rope. As he reached for the rock ledge, the anchor came undone and the rope gave way, losing its tension. Pete and the soldier with him gasped.

Dave lunged for the ledge and grabbed it as the rope flopped past him to the ground below. Pete ducked as the rope cascaded down. He looked up and wanted to cry out, but dared not. Dave struggled to maintain his grip on the icy ledge. Pete thought about trying to catch him or break his fall somehow, but he knew there was no chance, with his injured ankle. Dave was losing his grip.

Then, somehow, Dave held on, his feet dangling freely below him. Grunting, he swung his feet up on top, rolled over the lip, and collapsed near the cliff's edge, gasping loudly.

Barely audible, Pete said, "He did it. That son of a bitch did it."

The celebration was brief. They had lost enough time already and still had to reattach the rope.

"Well done, Dave. We've got to throw the rope up to you so you can re-anchor it. We'll drive the pitons back in place on the way up."

"Okay, Pete. Just let me sit up and get my bearings."

Impatient, Pete removed his bandolier strap, took out half the rounds to reduce its weight, and tied it to the end of the rope, to give it enough weight to toss it high enough. He handed it to the soldier next to him.

"Just toss it up there. The clock's ticking."

The other soldier, named Voelkelt, a stocky man with a boyish face and thick back who smelled vaguely of oatmeal, heaved the heavy strap and its attached rope up over the top of the twenty-foot cliff. It sailed over Dave, then dropped with a thud. Dave disappeared from sight for a few minutes, then returned, and gave a thumbs-up.

"I got her re-anchored up here. Whenever you're ready, head on up."

Voelkelt looked at Pete, who was sitting on the ground. "I know the lieutenant wants us to wait for everyone else and be the last ones up the rope, but they should've been here by now. I think we should go."

"Let's go, brother," Pete said. "The Krauts aren't going to hand us the summit, once they know we're up here. You're going to have to go before me and drive those pitons back in place. Then I'll follow."

"Can you make it on one leg?"

"I hope so. I've trained hard for so long; I don't think I could handle the disappointment of not doing this."

Voelkelt nodded somberly. "Higher," he said quietly.

"Higher," Pete replied.

The man scrambled up the rope, quickly drove the loose pitons back into the rock, and was over the top. Pete got up, balancing himself on his good leg. His muscles were stiff, and he was cold. He grabbed the rope and started climbing. It was harder than he anticipated, and he went slowly. He was only halfway up and already breathing hard. He had trouble looking for footholds.

"Come on, Pete, this is a cakewalk for you," Dave called down.

"The hell it is! I can't see the damn footholds!"

Near the top Pete lost his balance and wrapped his arms around the rope as his good foot slipped, leaving him dangling. The thought of plunging down and smacking into the ground, just like the body of the German he'd killed, flashed across his mind. He gritted his teeth, gripped the rope more tightly, and searched the rock frantically with the toe of his boot. He found a tiny protrusion, edged his sole on it, and pulled himself higher. His muscles burned as his heart raced. He pulled himself toward the edge of the wall, where Dave and Voelkelt waited. They grabbed him by the belt of his pants and yanked him up and over. All three collapsed in a pile on the rocky ground.

Dave and Voelkelt scrambled to their feet, grabbed their weapons, and searched the darkness. Recovering, Pete lay on the ground. The sound of soldiers on the trail down below drifted upward. Pete rose to his feet. Balancing uneasily, he grabbed his M1 rifle and limped toward the summit. He turned halfway round as he walked on. "Let's take the summit!"

"Let's wait for the lieutenant and the rest of the platoon. We'll take this thing in force," Dave said.

"I'm not getting left behind. I don't think the Krauts know we're here, but by the time they do, I intend to be on that damn summit." Pete trudged on.

"Ah hell, wait up," Dave called to him. "That field up there looks like it's nothing but loose rock, and you're going to stumble all over the place."

Pete kept walking, and Dave and the other soldier were by his side a moment later. He turned to Dave. "You're right, that field up ahead is nothing but loose rock."

"How do you know for certain?"

"I've been up here once already and froze my butt off then too."

"So what can we expect when we get there?"

All three men picked their way over loose, fist-sized rocks. Pete struggled, moving very cautiously, and Dave and Voelkelt slowed to match his pace.

"Unless things have changed somehow, we shouldn't expect much. The Krauts weren't even occupying the summit. We figured their command post must be somewhere down the western side of the mountain."

"Are you sure?"

"Hell, Dave, I'm not sure of anything. But we know Jerry is sending out patrols from somewhere on the mountain. Of *that* I am sure."

"How do you know the Krauts are sending out patrols?"

Pete stopped and looked at Dave full on, the shadow of his helmet draped across his face. "I just know." Then, just as abruptly, he turned and hobbled on.

About halfway up the scree field the trio paused to let Pete catch his breath and rest his ankle. Suddenly there was movement below. The three men turned, weapons ready. Thankfully, it was only the rest of the platoon advancing toward them from below. With Lieutenant Loose in the lead the platoon moved fast en masse over the loose rocks. Pete breathed more easily. His watch read 2:57 a.m.

"Let's keep going," Pete said.

"How's your ankle?" Voelkelt asked.

"It hurts like a son of a bitch. Let's go."

Pete did his best to move faster, his face a constant grimace. As he stumbled along, his lame foot slipped here and there, tweaking his swollen ankle repeatedly. The trio worked its way through the rest of the scree field and was overtaken by their comrades a hundred meters or so from the upper edge.

"How's your ankle?" Lieutenant Loose asked.

"Hurts like hell, works like shit, sir."

"Summit as quickly as you can, McGregor. Find me when you get there." He turned to the rest of the men behind him. "Let's keep moving. According to our reconnaissance the summit is about four hundred meters beyond the edge of this scree field. It should be lightly defended, if at all."

The platoon moved past Pete and disappeared into the fog, including the private who'd accompanied Pete so far. Only Dave stayed behind. Pete thanked him and traipsed on.

A short distance past the scree field a grenade exploded just below

Pete and Dave. They dropped to the ground and clung to their rifles. Then several more explosions rang out from below.

"I think those are German grenades, Dave."

Dave shook his head, looking unsure. Then more explosions followed. This time the sound was above them, somewhere in the fog. Then there was shouting, followed by single rifle shots and muffled machine gun bursts.

"Let's get moving, Dave!"

Pete and Dave moved up the mountain. Dave crouched low, and Pete did his best to copy him, but he struggled.

The firefight was closer now, within a hundred meters or so. Pete knew he was just below the obscured summit, and that the rest of the platoon was somewhere ahead. Dave was next to him, but slightly in front. They could only see fog, and pressed farther in. Pete felt the whir of a bullet as it whizzed by. He dropped to the ground, as did Dave.

Something clanked off the rocks and bounced toward Pete. It was what they called a potato masher—a German grenade. It lay just a few feet in front of him, with its long wooden handle and cylindrical, black head. Pete was frozen with terror. Then he covered up as best he could.

"No!" Dave shouted.

He lunged through the air, crashed onto the rock in front of Pete, snatched the grenade, rolled over, and whipped it down the slope. Both men covered up as the grenade exploded harmlessly off some rocks below.

Pete's breaths were labored and quick. His hands shook as he searched for his rifle, grabbed it, and tried to get up on shaky legs. He fell over.

"Easy, Pete, just wait a second. Get your composure."

More sounds of exchanged gunfire echoed from above. Then it grew sporadic and distant.

Pete climbed to his feet. Weakly he said, "Thanks, brother. I owe you one."

"The hell you do. We're in this mess together."

They pressed on, reached the summit in a crouch, and listened. Boots crunched along the ground a short distance away, but they still couldn't see much. Both men quickly deduced that the platoon had probably fanned out west, just off the Campiano's summit. Lieutenant Loose was expanding his perimeter, they were certain. The Tenth Mountain Division was now in possession of the Pizzo di Campiano, if only momentarily.

Pete took a drink of his grappa.

"You're hitting the sauce, Pete?"

"After what we just went through? Hell, I need *something*."

"Yeah, you do, but that ain't it."

Pete and Dave found Lieutenant Loose just to the south and west of the Campiano's summit. He was already at work establishing a tiny, crude command post.

"Ah, you made it, McGregor. Good. Like I told you, we need all the help we can get up here. And same to you, Bates."

"Where do you want us, Lieutenant?" Dave asked.

"Okay, men, listen. The Krauts should be to our west and north, somewhere down the mountain. I want both of you on our northern perimeter but on the eastern flank. You two will be the end of our line. Nobody gets around you. Understand?

"Jerry knows we're here now, and they'll come and try to kick us off. Stay together. You'll need each other to stay warm. Huddle under a blanket and put some dry socks on. And find Sergeant Lamb. He's somewhere on the northern perimeter as well, setting up our defensive line. Tell him my orders—that you two are to anchor the east end of our line. Go."

"Yes, sir," Pete and Dave responded.

As they headed out, Loose called after them. "*Nobody* gets around you. You're holding our eastern flank. Got it?"

"We got it, Lieutenant," Pete said.

They found the sergeant, who directed them to a spot roughly fifty meters east of two soldiers at the end of the line. Lamb lit a cigar, puffed out a cloud of gray, sweet smoke, and walked off to check on the rest of the northern perimeter. Other men, in tandem as well, were spread out among the barren rocks in a line that ran roughly east and west. There were four other duos to the west, and then the line turned south at a right angle. Pete and Dave walked to the eastern edge of the line. The scree field they had just come up was somewhat visible now down below.

Both men piled rocks, building a primitive wall that faced north and curved slightly west. Pete struggled to be of use. His ankle was weak and tender, and it throbbed. Dave forced him to sit and keep watch while he worked on their low wall. Pete piled a few rocks as best he could while sitting on the cold, misshapen heap. He pulled his blanket over himself, wedged his M1 between two larger rocks, and scanned the horizon to the north and west. Dave finished the wall and huddled on Pete's right under the blanket with him, facing directly north, his rifle ready as well.

Pete shivered and took another swig from his flask. He closed his eyes, savoring the warmth. The face of the dead German flashed in his mind, and he opened his eyes quickly, shivering again.

"How you doin', Pete?"

"Ankle hurts. I'm cold and hungry. I could use a hot shower. And that damn Kraut won't get out of my head. Other than that . . ."

"What Kraut?"

Pete closed his eyes and tried to rub the exhaustion out of his unshaven face.

"Crap, I thought I told you."

"You didn't tell me."

Pete stared into the darkness and thought he saw dark, moving shapes. He waited. Nothing moved; it was only rocks.

"I killed a Kraut."

"When?"

"When we came up here on patrol and attached the ropes, a few weeks ago."

"So *that's* how you knew about the Germans sending out patrols on the Campiano, huh?"

Pete nodded and glanced sharply at Dave, then turned away. The night was still. A rock clacked against another somewhere to the left. It was almost four o'clock in the morning.

"I don't trust the Krauts, Dave. They've got something cooking. It's too calm."

"I agree, Pete. But we can only wait."

"I'm afraid you're right. Hey, I'm sorry for not telling you about the guy I killed. He was just a kid, you know?" Pete's throat tightened. "He was expendable…just like us, I guess." He tried to wipe away his tears as casually as he could.

"Not much younger than us."

Pete could only nod, too overcome. Moments later he finally spoke.

He told Dave about fixing the rope. "This poor German bastard was just out on patrol trying to do his job, ya know?"

Pete struggled to go on.

"I can't get his face out of my head. I strangled him to death, Dave. And…I can see his face, all twisted, his tongue, his lifeless eyes staring back at me. I can still smell him too."

Pete closed his eyes again, breathing hard, his voice choking.

"We had to hide the body, so we rolled him off the trail into the ravine. Poor guy. His fat German mother will keep writing to him, with no idea her son is dead."

Tears came slowly.

"I'm sorry, Pete."

Pete pulled out another chocolate bar, broke off a section, and handed it to Dave. He was very hungry now. He felt inside the pockets of his jacket and pants. He had one more chocolate bar and a package of crackers with cheese, but nothing else. He sipped from his canteen, trying to conserve his water, which was almost completely gone. He munched on a few crackers, hoping to stem the pangs in his stomach. He shot a glance at Dave.

"Thanks, Dave."

"For what?"

"For what you did with that grenade."

Then there was whispering, and Pete perked up for a moment, gripping his rifle tighter. But it was only some of his comrades, down the line to his left. He took a quick sip of grappa. "Why'd you do it, Dave? Why did you go after that grenade?"

Dave stared at the ground, as though he was examining one of the innumerable, plain, gray rocks that covered the summit.

"Some of it was instinct."

Dave pressed his lips together tight and seemed to struggle to choose the right words. Then he raised his head and turned to Pete. "I didn't love my wife well. I think a husband should pour out his life for his wife. But in the time since she died, I've come to realize that a real man pours out his life for those who need it. And you needed it when that grenade landed at your feet."

Pete stared back, his eyes burning deep in the shadows of his helmet. He felt small. He still held his M1 tight, then reached for his flask again with his trigger-finger hand, and took another sip. Its warmth disappeared quickly, and he was cold again.

"Thanks," was all that Pete could say, unable now to look at Dave. He'd never felt this kind of love from another human being, and it humbled and shamed him. Choked with emotion, he struggled to ask, "Did you do it because of your faith?"

"Yes. This is the kind of love God asks of those who put their trust in Him. But I never really understood this until after Lucy died." Dave's voice was thick with emotion. Dave wiped his nose on his jacket sleeve.

Pete looked up.

"I learned it too late for my wife. I'm glad I didn't learn it too late for you."

There was nothing more to say, and each man knew it. Pete checked his watch. It was 4:30 a.m. Suddenly Pete sensed that something was wrong. It was too quiet. He was about to say something when a voice from the line said, "Look sharp. The Krauts are up to something."

Sure enough, the first German counterattack was under way. A dozen German soldiers moved toward the Americans' position. They came in from the north and west, out of the fog, in an attempt to outflank them. They were about a hundred meters away. Half of the enemy squad, to the left of Pete's and Dave's outpost, stopped and held their positions. The other half moved left to right in cohesion, like a pack of hungry wolves. Pete's hands were sweaty inside his gloves, and he tried to hold his rifle tighter, fearing it might slip away somehow at this crucial moment. He glanced over his shoulder; there was no one behind them. Lieutenant Loose's words rang in his head, "*Nobody* gets around you!" He was afraid, picturing Dave being shot, their position overrun, and German soldiers clubbing him to death with rifle butts.

"You see 'em, Pete?" Dave whispered.

"Yep."

"How close do you think we should let them get?"

"I'm not sure."

There had been no kind of signal or direction from Sergeant Lamb. Pete wished he had a Tommy gun.

The Germans were talking in hushed tones to each other. Pressure filled Pete's ears. He needed water, but he didn't dare move. The six Germans moved again in sync, coming closer. They were about seventy-five meters away now. Pete fingered his trigger guard and made sure his safety was off.

"Dave?" Pete whispered.

"Yeah?"

"Don't you think we should rise up a bit, when we're ready, and shoot over the wall? That way we can be more accurate."

"We'll be easier targets, Pete, but yeah, I think you're right."

The Germans moved closer again, another few meters, in unison. Pete slowly backed his M1 out from between the rocks to be ready to shoot over the wall. He tried to position his body, worrying about his ankle giving way. Sweat trickled down his chest. He licked his cracked lips.

"Okay, Pete, I'll aim for the three guys on the right, you take the three on the left."

"Okay," Pete said, almost with a squeak.

Slowly, cautiously, Dave said, "On three. Here we go. One, two...three."

In unison, Pete and Dave rose up into a half-kneeling position and opened fire, a high-pitch ringing filling their ears.

The M1 recoiled into Pete's shoulder. Small sparks ricocheted off the rocks. Everything seemed blurry and moving too fast, but he kept firing.

Pete wounded a German, who rolled over screaming in pain and grabbing his shoulder. Then there were flashes to his right. A German had sprung up, unleashing a burst of automatic fire toward Pete, causing sparks on the rocks in front of the wall. Pete hit the ground hard, looking for cover. He banged his knee and his knuckles in the process, but the pain didn't register.

Keep your head down! What the hell's the matter with you?!

He tried to see the gunner through the rocks, but he couldn't. Dave was hunkered down, too, his back to Pete. They were pinned down. Sporadic support fire opened up, off to their left, from some of their own men. Dave crouched with his rifle ready. He popped up fast and glanced over the wall.

"Grenade!" he shouted. "Get low!"

Then he dropped back down, collapsing on top of Pete. Pete tensed up.

The grenade exploded in front of the wall. Debris cascaded down and peppered both men with tiny bits of rock.

"Hell, Dave, we gotta keep that bastard away from us! I'll toss a grenade!"

Pete pulled a grenade from his pocket and waited to pull the pin.

Dave sprang up and fired off three quick rounds.

Dave had used up his magazine, and the empty container caromed out of his rifle and bounced around the rocks below. Then he dropped down again, his chest heaving.

"I...I think I wounded him. He's about twenty meters in front of us. I gotta reload."

"How the hell did he get so close?"

"Just throw the damn grenade, Pete!"

Pete pulled the pin on his grenade and rose up fast. He saw a huddled figure a short distance from their wall. A burst of machine gun fire rattled away to his left and ricocheted off the rocks. Pete hunched his shoulders, lobbed the grenade, and ducked back down.

"Fire in the hole!"

There was a sudden, hollow explosion followed by pieces of shrapnel ricocheting off the rocks in every direction.

It was quiet for a moment. Dave peered over the wall. The machine gun opened up again, and Dave plopped back down. There were rifle shots now too.

"We gotta take that son of a bitch out, Dave!"

"No shit!"

Suddenly there was a clanking on the rocks behind them. Pete turned around. A small, black shape bounced around.

"Grenade!"

Both men covered up.

The explosion came quickly. Suddenly there was a sharp burning in Pete's calf.

"Damn it! I'm hit!"

Pete writhed about, then the pain dulled slightly.

"That's it, Dave! I've had enough. Load up. We're taking that bastard out, even if . . ."

Dave sprang up and emptied the magazine of his rifle, swinging his M1 back and forth quickly and precisely, sending bullets in every direction. Then he dropped back down.

"I got him!"

"You think so?"

Pete and Dave waited. There was only irregular rifle fire now. Pete pushed himself up so that his helmet was just above the wall. The three remaining soldiers retreated, bounding over the rocks, back the way they'd come, into the darkness of a patch of dwarf-like trees to the north. Then he collapsed behind the wall again, still out of breath. His boot was wet and squishy inside.

"Take a look at my leg, will ya, Dave?"

Dave peered over the wall one last time and scanned the rocks, then ducked back down. He pulled out his knife and split Pete's pant leg open.

"There's a lot of blood. Are you in a lot of pain?"

"It's not too bad. Maybe it's just a flesh wound."

"I think you're right, which is good because we may as well be on the Moon when it comes to getting you to a field hospital."

Pete was shot in the calf, but the bullet appeared to have passed through cleanly, leaving an entry and exit hole, a lot of blood, and an uncomplicated wound.

"Just throw some sulfa on it and dress it for me."

Dave sterilized the wound with sulfa powder, then bandaged it tightly. Pete's calf throbbed, and he swallowed a handful of aspirin. Dave offered to keep watch, and Pete lay down on the rocks with his back against the wall. He elevated his leg and tried to sleep but couldn't, so he sat up and kept watch too.

The day was breaking, and the fog took on a faint glow. It comforted Pete. His courage returned in a small way. He had a splash of water left in his canteen. He ate his last chocolate bar but decided to save his crackers until he could scrounge water somewhere. Sometime later Sergeant Lamb paid them a visit, telling them that since they had more men on top now, their line would be fortified. Pete asked if he had any water, and Lamb looked at him like he was nuts. Then the sergeant grabbed his canteen and poured a small amount into Pete's. He moved off west, then south toward the command post, and came back twenty minutes later with three more two-man teams in tow. He placed one to the immediate left of Pete and Dave, about twenty-five meters away.

"Dave, can you find me some more water?"

"Can you go without it?"

"I don't think so. I'm so hungry my stomach hurts, and if I eat my crackers, I'll need some water. I'd go myself, but I can hardly use my leg now."

Dave grabbed Pete's canteen, glanced north into the fog, then leaped across the rocks to the newly arrived duo. He wasn't gone long. Then he tossed the canteen into Pete's lap.

Later that morning the Germans counterattacked again, this time more to the west. Pete and Dave saw a few enemy soldiers to their distant left. They waited, their weapons ready, for more enemy soldiers to appear in front of their own position. The sound of exchanged rifle shots, occasional bursts of automatic fire, and exploding grenades echoed across the rocks. Pete was glad they'd been spared, for the moment, of more combat.

"War isn't like I thought it would be," he blurted out.

Dave said nothing, so Pete turned to look at him. He stared

blankly back. Pete felt embarrassed and regretted what he'd said; he felt obliged to explain himself.

"I didn't realize how frightening it would be. I guess that sounds stupid, as though it should have been obvious. Killing that German was a helluva thing. Seeing those lifeless eyes. Nuts. I just want to clean up this shitty mess and get the hell home."

"I agree with you. How will we ever be able to tell someone about all this?"

The nearby combat continued. Dave glanced in that direction, worry splashed across his face. Then he was up and moving toward it. Over his shoulder he shouted back, "Just hold the line, Pete! Sing out if you need help!"

Dave moved fast. He ran low, stopping at the next pair of fellow soldiers. He said something, then moved off into the fog, further west.

Pete held the platoon's eastern flank all by himself now. His senses grew sharper, and his muscles, more tense. His mouth went dry. He sipped from his flask again, which was almost out.

Ah hell, it's hard to see anything. I have two injuries now, and if the Krauts want to overrun me, they can do it pretty easily.

He peered over the wall, looking north. A German lay on the rocks in the distance, not moving. He turned away quickly. To the west shots rang out back and forth, and there was shouting. But there were less grenade explosions now.

Pete's mind played tricks on him. *I really want to know what's going on. There's nothing out there right now, or is that someone moving in the fog? Is that one of theirs or one of ours? Damn it! Who is that?*

"Dave!" Pete shouted into the mist. "Is that you, Dave?"

Shit, that's a Kraut!

"Thunder!" Pete called out.

He waited for the correct response. Nothing.

"Thunder!" he said again.

Still no response.

Pete fired into the gray. He waited and fired another round. It was quiet again. Suddenly Dave's voice drifted over to his left from out of the gray. Dave bumbled back over the rocks, going more slowly this time. Pete signaled for him to hurry up and stay low. He dropped down next to Pete.

"What's going on, Pete?"

"I think Jerry is trying to outflank us."

"You see someone?"

"Yeah, I think so. There's some Kraut out there, maybe more, just to our north, somewhere in the fog. I think he's trying to sneak by me. I fired a few shots."

Dave knelt and gazed over the wall, his helmet hovering just above it. He squinted, straining to see something. Then he dropped back down.

"I don't see a thing, Pete."

"But what if he really is out there? What if he sneaks up, surprises us, and machine-guns everyone to death? That one guy could fold our flank and enable the Germans to retake the summit."

"Okay. Stay here and cover me. I'll go take a look. Don't shoot me!"

Dave grabbed his rifle, crouched low, and slipped around the end of the rock wall. Pete watched closely, his rifle ready. Dave disappeared into the fog. Minutes crept by.

I think he's been out there for a half-hour, Pete thought. *Crap, maybe he's in trouble. Should I go? Would I be abandoning my post? Damn it!*

Pete struggled to his feet and walked carefully around the wall, clicking his M1 off safety. He caught the attention of the two men down the line from him, and signaled that he was heading forward and for them to stay put. He wandered toward the fog, shaking. He saw a gray figure coming low toward him.

That's a German uniform!

He knelt and raised his rifle.

"Thunder!"

"Flash!" came the reply. It was Dave.

Pete clicked his safety back on and lowered his rifle.

"Shit, Dave, I thought you were a Kraut! I could've sworn you had a gray uniform on. Be careful! Anyway, what'd you find?"

"There's nothing out there, Pete. I think Jerry has given up on the old end-around for the moment."

Pete and Dave walked back to the wall and took up their positions.

"Oh, I almost forgot," Dave said. "Give me your canteen. I got you more water."

Dave filled Pete's canteen to half.

"So, what happened earlier, Dave?"

"The Krauts tried to go straight up the gut. Fullback up the middle, ya know?"

He handed Pete the canteen, sipped from his own, capped it, and threw it down on the rocks in disgust.

"Those poor guys got creamed. What a waste."

Toward evening Pete's calf was throbbing again. He gulped more aspirin. It didn't work. And the pain in his swollen calf grew worse when he tried to walk. He was stuck.

Sergeant Lamb informed Pete and Dave that Lieutenant Loose, believing he'd located the vicinity of the German command post, needed a dozen men to go on a spoiling attack later that night. Dave volunteered immediately. He and Pete pooled their ammo together for him. All Pete could do was watch him disappear into the dark.

Pete was out of water now, and it seemed the throbbing from his calf had traveled to his brain as well. His lame ankle wasn't much better. He couldn't get his mind off his wounds and his thirst.

He checked the north: nothing. So he got up and hobbled over to the next men in the line. He'd seen them using one of the division's small mountain stoves earlier. He asked to borrow the stove so he could melt snow. They handed it to him, and he thanked them, telling them to stay sharp and that he was going to collect some snow for melting. He wandered over to the eastern edge of the summit and saw a patch of snow a few meters down, wedged between a few larger rocks. Carefully he made his way down to it. It was old snow, crusty and crystalline.

Dang corn snow. Probably been here since Christmas.

He scooped what he could into his steel helmet and tried to pack some more into the small top of his canteen, but the snow was too brittle. He limped back to his rocky perch at the end of the line. He lit the little stove, the heat wonderful and comforting. His thoughts drifted to skiing with Dave, to being in Colorado, and to Camp

Hale. He missed Dave, even now, though he'd only been gone a short while.

He held his helmet over the burner, blue flames dancing along the bottom. He pulled out his empty flask and licked the cap and the threads. His food was long gone too.

"Where the hell is our damn relief?" he cursed softly.

There's nothing to do but wait. A watched pot never boils, brother.

He tried to smile but couldn't.

"Okay, McGregor, toughen up," he told himself. "Get a hold of yourself. Try to think about something else. Let's think about Dave. What is different about Dave? Is Dave different, or am I? Why do I feel naked without him?"

A tiny pool of water began to form in his helmet.

The German he'd killed intruded into his thoughts again. Like a movie reel in his head, he watched the body being rolled off the cliff, followed by the sickening thud below. His thoughts jumped around, and suddenly he had his arm around the German's neck and could smell his shaving soap. Then there was the quick snap of the enemy soldier's neck and the body limp and heavy against him.

Pete pushed down tears as well as the need to vomit. Half the snow in his helmet was liquid now. Pete wanted to drink, but he decided to wait.

"I could've had a nice career in shipping, suits, a Cadillac, endless girls, dinners, parties, martinis. What the hell was I thinking?"

You need more, Pete, a voice in his head said. *That stuff isn't enough for you.*

"Yeah, but it would've been fun to discover the answer for myself," he said to no one.

But then what? Become like your father? No, that isn't the life I want, but what is?

Most of the snow had melted by now. Pete grabbed his canteen, knelt, wedged it between his legs, and pulled his helmet off the burner. A wave of heat leapt up, caressing his face. He poured the water carefully into the small opening of his canteen, spilled some, and cursed at how little had been produced. He put his helmet on and held his face over the burner for a moment longer, a faint smile on his lips. Then he turned it off. He only took a sip, then another, followed by one more. Half his water was already gone now. He scolded himself, made another painful trip back to the patch of old snow, and repeated the process.

This time he conserved his water, returned the stove to his comrades, and limped back to his place in the line. He hadn't carried his rifle with him, walking upright and slow there in the dark; he no longer cared whether the enemy saw him or not.

Suddenly someone was coming, from the north and west. Pete grabbed his rifle, fingered the safety off, and brushed the trigger with his finger. It was Dave again.

Pete relaxed a little, sighing. But something wasn't right. Then he knew why. Dave's upper pant leg was split open, and his thigh was wrapped in a bandage. There was a dark spot on the white gauze. Dave walked gingerly over to Pete, sat down behind the wall, and leaned against it. His face was pale and creased. He laid his rifle down and wiped his brow.

"What the hell happened to you?"

He told Pete how they headed toward the vicinity of the German line, then came across an earthen dugout. Lieutenant Loose signaled for the four men up front, Dave being one of them, to break down the door and toss a few grenades inside.

Dave paused in his recounting, tilted his helmet back, and mopped his brow again as he sipped from his canteen. Then he resumed with his story.

They were about to open the door when six Germans filed out, who saw the Americans and charged. Dave shot one of the soldiers, while another German machine-gunned an American soldier to death. Dave dropped his rifle and lunged at the killer with his knife. He struggled against the taller German soldier but managed to stab him to death, though not before getting knifed in his thigh.

Dave set his canteen down, scrounged in his pockets, and pulled out a piece of cheese.

"I can't eat this. You take it," he said, and handed it to Pete. He wiped his nose on the sleeve of his field jacket. "Like you said, it's a helluva thing to kill someone, especially up close."

Pete took off his helmet and stared at the inside of it. He felt his throat tighten and his stomach churn. He turned to the side and heaved, but nothing came out. His stomach convulsed again. Still nothing came out. He sat up and fumbled for his water, still holding the piece of cheese Dave had given him.

"What happened next?"

"The other three Krauts surrendered. We took them back to the CP."

"That's all the men who were in there?"

Dave nodded.

"We think there are a lot more, but I guess they were out on patrol."

"Or they're preparing for another attack."

Dave shrugged.

"We searched the place and found a briefcase with documents, a mortar, and a couple of machine guns. One was an MG34. Oh, and we found some food too: a few loaves of stale bread and some cheese and chocolate. Which reminds me . . ."

Dave reached in his jacket pocket. He pulled out a bar of German chocolate and handed it to Pete.

"I know you're starving. Sorry I didn't remember to give it to you sooner."

"You keep it. I'm not sure I can hold it down."

"Save it for later then. I have another one, and I ate a hunk of the bread."

"How's your leg, Dave?"

"Hurts like a son of a bitch. Lamb dressed it—did a good job, too, but the bandage is so tight it's making my leg throb. How are you doing?"

Pete shrugged, passing his hand through his short, greasy hair.

"My life sure didn't turn out the way I thought it would."

"Mine didn't either, Pete."

Pete put his helmet back on, grabbed his M1, and peered over the wall into the night fog.

A shot rang out to the west and south. The fog suffocated the sound quickly.

"Do you regret your life, Dave?"

"I think I used to."

"What changed?"

"I failed Lucy, but I'm learning from that failure. And that makes me hopeful."

Pete managed a weak smile. "I've failed a lot too. I guess I've never realized that sometimes failure can be a good thing."

"If we let it, yeah. Lucy probably would've been glad."

It was the middle of the night, and Pete fell asleep where he sat, his hands on his rifle and his head poking out from beneath the blanket he shared with Dave. He woke up and lifted his head from the rocks, unsure where he was for a moment. There was Dave, still next to him, keeping watch and holding the end of the line in the dawn gloom.

"Why don't you try to sleep, Dave? You must be exhausted."

"Who isn't?"

"I'll take watch. Try to grab a few winks."

"That sounds good. Keep an eye peeled. Jerry's been too quiet for too long. Do you have any grenades left?"

"I'm out."

"Yeah, me too. I'm also out of food and almost out of water. How's your ammo?"

"I'm almost out. I still can't believe we haven't been relieved. I'd love to know what the hell the division is doing down there."

"I agree, Pete. If they don't get us some help soon, we'll lose the summit."

Pete nodded, stood up cautiously, and stretched the night from his aching body. He turned to Dave to ask him a question, but his friend was already asleep. Later that morning a wind blew up and dispersed the fog.

By now it had been almost two days, and the Second Platoon still hadn't been relieved. Pete and Dave, with the rest of their fellow soldiers, had now run out of everything except ammunition. Pete had been up all day, no longer able to find sleep among the rocks. His calf throbbed, and when he checked the wound, he saw streaks of red beginning to appear on his skin. Hunger pangs rumbled through his belly, and his mouth was cottony and sticky. His eyes stung, and the cold, steady wind made it worse.

But he felt better when he was near Dave. He knew Dave was as cold, tired, hungry, and thirsty as he was, and Dave's wounded leg was no better than his injured leg either. Still, Dave didn't gripe.

Dave has definitely changed, Pete thought. *Life is shitty right now, but he's weightless somehow, like he's unburdened by it.*

Dave took his turn on watch around midnight, and Pete tried to sleep. Dave shook him from a black, empty slumber. Pete looked at his watch. It was two a.m. on the twentieth. He fumbled for something before he realized he was looking for his rifle. He was mad with thirst, mumbling that he was going to look for some snow for his canteen.

"Shh! There's no time for that crap. Take your safety off. We got a whole mess of Krauts coming. I can see and hear 'em."

"What? From where?"

"They're coming in from the north, maybe eighty to a hundred meters out. There's a small grove of trees over there, and I can hear their voices coming from inside them. They're probably using it as a staging area. I think this is it. I think they're going to try to roll our flank."

Dave signaled to the two men to their left, letting them know what he saw. They nodded in affirmation.

"Dave, someone should go tell Sergeant Lamb our situation so he can radio the lieutenant."

"I agree."

Suddenly, like magic, Sergeant Lamb appeared among the rocks, running low and hard and coming straight toward Pete and Dave. He almost bowled Pete over, slamming into him like he was being chased by the devil himself. Lamb held on to his helmet, breathing hard. He held a walkie-talkie in the other hand, with his carbine slung over his shoulder.

"What do we got?" he practically yelled.

"Krauts coming in, Sarge," Dave said, "from the north, 'bout eighty meters away."

"Yeah, we saw a few of them moving past us, headed your way. I figured I'd check up on you guys. How many have you seen?"

"None, but we can hear their voices," Pete said.

Suddenly numerous dark shapes emerged from the grove of trees. Like a swarm they came closer. They moved nonstop, crawling, running, crouching, running some more. Clanking echoed through the air from the enemy's equipment rustling and their boots treading on the rocks.

Pete thought he heard the cocking of a machine gun bolt. He counted quickly—well over a dozen enemy soldiers now. His heart raced, and he sweated in the cold.

"Hell, that's a lot of men," Lamb said.

He seemed to be running numbers in his head.

"We're not enough. Damn, we're not enough. We need more men. We have seven guys against, what, fifteen, maybe twenty Krauts? That's two or three to one. We'll never hold. Damn!"

Suddenly shots erupted everywhere. Sparks flew in all directions as a torrent of automatic and rifle fire descended like a cloudburst. Pete, Dave, and Sergeant Lamb cowered behind the wall of stones, pressing into the rocks as best they could. Bullets whizzed by like angry hornets. Intermittent pops from the American side responded, but the effort was paltry.

A machine gun opened up, but it sounded different to Pete. It wasn't the staccato of a typical automatic weapon. This was a loud, constant, metallic-like ripping. And suddenly Pete knew. It was a powerful MG42 machine gun. It fired twice the amount of rounds of a typical American machine gun.

German soldiers, in their camouflage smocks, flowed over the hard landscape and came on. Pete panicked, his thoughts racing. He held onto his helmet and rifle, cringing from the enemy's fury.

Sergeant Lamb radioed Lieutenant Loose, yelling above the din.

"Lieutenant! Lieutenant!"

Lamb waited, then screamed back, "We need some artillery right now!"

Lamb listened, then shouted, "We'll clear out! Just call it in, Lieutenant! This flank's gonna fold if we don't get fire support immediately!"

Lamb listened again, then responded to Lieutenant Loose with their coordinates for the artillery. He added, "Give me a few minutes to clear everyone out, then call it in!"

Lamb turned to Pete and Dave. "All right, you guys, we're outta here. Stay on my ass! We're gonna head back down the line. We'll pick up our comrades as we go."

Lamb signaled to the next men over to provide covering fire. Due to their injuries, he'd have to place an arm around Pete and Dave and help them along, back down the line.

"No." Dave said, abruptly. "The three of us will never make it. That MG42 will cut us to ribbons. And you can't support both of us, Sarge. I'll stay and provide covering fire."

"No way, Dave!" Pete shouted. "I'm not leaving without you. Just come. We've got a chance of making it. You can't stay. You can't survive a direct artillery barrage."

"*All* of us can't make it, Pete, and you know it. Ask Sarge. He knows I'm right."

"I hate to say it, but he's right," Lamb said.

No one said anything. There was only the intrusion of the war, brusque and unyielding.

Finally Lamb said, "Let's go, McGregor. None of us will probably make it anyway, but this is the only way we have some sort of a chance. I'm sorry."

Lamb turned to Dave.

"I'll try to come back for you."

"Okay."

Everyone knew it couldn't be so.

Pete's head was down, as were Dave's and Sergeant Lamb's, all still cowering from the enemy's deadly, ubiquitous fire. A hand grenade exploded behind them south of their rock pile, peppering them with bits of rock and ice. Pete's eyes filled with tears, and he couldn't speak. He grabbed Dave's arm. He squeezed hard, unable to let go.

"It'll be okay, Pete, somehow. Learn to have faith. Give of yourself to those who need it. It's what men do. It'll all work out for good, buddy."

Lamb grabbed Pete. "We gotta go, McGregor, right now! I'll come back for him."

The sergeant wrapped his arm around Pete's back and held onto his arm, which was draped across the sergeant's neck. Sergeant Lamb and Dave nodded at each other. Then Dave popped up, just over the parapet, and unloaded the magazine of his M1, punchy shots coming one after the other.

Pete and Sergeant Lamb sprang to life. They stumbled across the rocks as fast as they could, heads down. Bullets were everywhere, bouncing off the rocks. The MG42 split the air in a cacophony of deadly steel. Pete winced, waiting for its bullets to crash into his body and fold him to the ground. The pop of Dave's M1 rang back in defiance. Pete tried to steal a glance back at Dave, but Lamb, moving hard and fast, gripped him too tight to allow it.

They reached the next pair of soldiers in the line, who were firing at the attacking Germans as well.

Lamb screamed, "Move out! Shells coming in! Let's go!"

Pain shot through Pete's ankle and calf, travelled up his leg, then engulfed his whole body. Head down, he saw only the rocks as they passed in a blur beneath his shaky, clumsy legs.

Suddenly Lamb let go, and both men tumbled onto the rocks. The sergeant's body lay heavily against Pete, unmoving. Pete struggled to roll the sergeant off him. Bullets pummeled Lamb's lifeless body.

"Sarge!" Pete screamed. "Sarge!"

Cold, vacant eyes stared back.

Just then the artillery barrage crashed in. The long, friendly whine of the American guns brought relief as well as dread. Earth-shaking explosions erupted all over the landscape.

Pete ducked, trying his best to hold his helmet on and get as low as he could. Then he pulled Lamb's body on top of his own, desperate for protection.

"Sorry, Sarge!"

A shower of American artillery thundered down over the Campiano, smothering it like a giant wave. Bursts of white light ripped through the darkness. A round burst nearby. Its light blinded Pete just before the concussion knocked him out.

Pete woke up to an orangey eastern sky. He was at the platoon's command post, laid out on the rocks. A fresh dressing was on his leg, and his ankle was rewrapped. His head had been bandaged as well. Someone had shared some water with him. He tried to get up, but a medic pushed him back down. He was a wreck, but all he could think about was Dave. Did he survive? Was he lying here at the command post, too, wounded but not dead? He had to know.

"Just stay there, Private. We thought you were dead. You were bleeding out of your nose and ears when they brought you in. Those artillery rounds probably broke your eardrums."

Pete had trouble understanding him. All sounds were warped, distant. Pete waited until the medic wandered off, then sat up, dizzy. He stood up, the ground spun, and he collapsed. He managed to sit back up, then finished the water left in his canteen. Gingerly he put his helmet on over his bandaged head. He stood up again slowly. He saw his rifle lying on the ground nearby and managed to reach it and pick it up.

He glanced around the tiny command post hoping to find Dave. He wasn't there. Ignoring the medic's pleadings, he shuffled painfully back up to the line, toward the position he'd held with Dave. He tried to maintain discipline, staying low and moving as fast as his injuries would allow. But he quit before he was halfway to his post, in terrible pain and no longer caring if a German soldier placed a round or two in his head. But he didn't have to worry. After the artillery barrage, any effective German resistance on the summit of the Campiano ceased to exist.

He came to the remnants of the little stone wall he and Dave had occupied together. The stones were scattered now, scraped and broken. He slung his M1 over his shoulder and searched the rocks. There was nothing, not even a sign of Dave's helmet. He found the little place on the line where he guessed he and Dave had stood, and sat next to it.

He set his rifle down and took off his helmet. His boots caught his attention. They were scuffed, creased, and abused.

He reached down to adjust one of his laces, then saw something down between the stones. It was part of a necklace. There were two objects attached to it: a small metal cross, bent and twisted, and a piece of a dog tag. Pete looked closely. Most of the tag had been destroyed, ripped apart and scattered in all directions. It was impossible to determine exactly who the tag belonged to. He kissed it, along with the cross, then put both objects carefully in his jacket pocket. He put his helmet on, looking north over the remnants of the shattered wall, into enemy territory.

He wept.

18 - RESCUE

Pete woke up in a daze, his head aching and spinning. Travis was shaking him. It was daylight, and gusts of cold air and snow whipped through the shelter, sometimes a friend and sometimes a foe to Pete's fevered body. The unsupported roof of their half-shelter sagged as the snow from the storm piled up on it.

"You were doing it again, Pete."

"Doing what?"

"You were shouting out names in your sleep."

"Travis, are you worried that we're close to death?"

"Yes."

Travis burst into sobs then, and just as quickly as his crying came, it was over. He wiped his tears away with a quick, determined, gloved hand.

Pete squirmed out of his sleeping bag and crawled the short distance to Travis, praying he didn't topple over while everything spun around him and as pangs stabbed his injured arm. He held Travis's hands between his own and searched the young man's eyes. "It'll be okay, Travis. God has a plan. Learn to trust. I won't leave you, son." Then he, too, sobbed softly, and again a torrent of tears escaped from the young man.

"How the hell do you know it'll all be okay, Pete? You don't, do you? We're gonna die out here in the wilderness, like a couple of animals. I just know it."

Pete had no idea how long he'd comforted the young man. He couldn't really remember, either, crawling back to his sleeping bag. He'd swallowed a handful of pain pills, way past the recommended dosage, then forced down half a liter of water. Then he collapsed again, into a hellish, feverish twilight sleep.

Sometime during the night, in his latest, twisted dream, Pete had a vague notion that he was cold and wet, and getting more so the longer his dream lasted. Then suddenly he was awake, discovering a tiny avalanche of snow engulfing his body.

"Holy smokes!"

Suddenly Travis was awake too.

"What's wrong, Pete?"

"Our roof collapsed. I meant to get the snow off yesterday, and prop up the middle, but I was too feverish and exhausted. Nuts!"

Pete's head felt like an inferno, and he was nauseous. He put two fingers to his neck, to check his pulse. It was high, another sign of a staph infection. He inched himself free from his sleeping bag and brushed away as much of the snow as he could, pushing it toward the entrance, holding handfuls of snow against his forehead, trying to lower his temperature. Then everything started spinning, and he crawled toward the entrance before vomiting.

He had no choice but to clear their collapsed roof. And Travis was in no shape to help. So Pete did his best to scoop the snow off the tarp with his pack shovel. Spasms of pain shot through his wounded arm. It was swollen, too—another bad sign of his worsening infection.

Pete got the tarp cleared, as well as a portion of the snow choking the entrance to their shelter. Then he propped up the roof with a ski pole. His face was pelted when he went back out into the unrelenting wind and snow. He wanted to check each of the tarp's anchors. He checked the first and approached the second before collapsing.

When Pete woke, it was still dark, and he was facedown in the new snow. Vomit stained the snowy ground around his head, spread out in a violent, bursting fashion. Pete tried to collect his thoughts, directing them toward something concrete.

Get back under the tarp, McGregor!

He knew he needed to get back inside and tell Travis to follow the emergency plan. He needed to tell him where the fire paste and lighter were, and the morphine too. But he decided he'd have to inject the needle himself; that was too much to ask of Travis.

Pete crawled into the tent, desperate to plop down on his sleeping bag, curl it around himself, and wait for rescue or death, whichever came first. But he didn't. It took all his strength to stay upright, and he was terrified that if he lay down he wouldn't get back up before it was too late. He prayed nonstop as he found his headlamp and fished for his morphine kit, fire paste, and Zippo lighter.

"Our Father, who art in heaven, hallowed be Thy name . . ."

Pete tucked the morphine inside his jacket pocket, then searched for the paste and lighter.

"Thy kingdom come, Thy will be done, on Earth as it is in heaven . . ."

He found the paste and the lighter, kissed them, and dragged himself back out into the storm.

"Give us this day our daily bread, and forgive us our trespasses, as we forgive those who trespass against us . . ."

His whole body hurt, his joints achy and stiff. His head was burning up. The cold seemed to penetrate his body as though he had no clothes on. Shaking violently, he scanned the woods uphill looking for a suitable patch of pines. Unsure, he quickly gave up and trudged into the darkness, each leg sinking deep. He'd wanted to go fifty paces but lacked the strength and only made it twenty. He found a decent clump of conifers and grabbed the fire paste. He smeared the entire tube as high as he could, just under a few low-lying boughs.

"And lead us not into temptation, but deliver us from evil, for Thine is the kingdom, and the power, and the glory, forever. Amen."

He pulled out his old lighter and held it aloft, hoping it would light in the winter wind.

"Our Father, who art in heaven . . ."

A brief, bluish flame flickered a moment, then quickly disappeared.

"Hallowed be Thy name. Thy kingdom come, Thy will be done . . ."

He tried again and met the same result. Then again. Then a fourth time and a fifth. A whiff of lighter fluid caught his attention. He paused, then prayed over the lighter.

He cupped the Zippo, struck it, then held it aloft, as a yellowish flame sprang up and licked the paste, before the wind snuffed out the lighter again. But it was enough. Flames consumed the fire paste and rose into the branches as the wind whipped about, fanning and spreading them quickly. Pete watched for only a moment, craving the warmth but knowing he had to get a safe distance away. With all his remaining strength, he retraced his steps, pausing twice over the short distance to catch his breath.

At the entrance to the shelter he gazed back uphill. Orange flames danced about the lower branches of the tree, spreading and shooting skyward. He turned away and caught a glimpse of the eastern sky, wondering whether it was a shade brighter or just his fevered, exhausted mind playing tricks. Too tired to think about it, he knelt in the snow and pulled out a vial of morphine. With shaking hands and the world starting to spin again, he dropped his pants, tore off the wrapper with his teeth, and jammed the needle into his thigh. Then he pulled out another one and repeated the procedure. He had only one vial left. He tucked it safely away, yanked up his trousers, and crawled into the shelter. He lay down, his sleeping bag around him, his thoughts a wild, serpentine mix of God, his wife and kids, David Bates, and Travis. And death.

Pete woke, blinking in the artificial wash of fluorescent lights in the ceiling above. He tried to sit up, but a man in a blue uniform gently pushed him back down.

"Whoa, easy there, old-timer. Just stay put. I'm going to give you some oxygen. Then we'll get you to the hospital."

The man held a clear, plastic mask in his hand and moved it toward Pete's face.

"Wait. Wait a minute. Just tell me. What happened?"

"We found you earlier today, you and your son. You're in bad shape, but I think you'll be okay."

"Is…is he okay?"

"Your son? He'll make it out all right. You saved his life. He owes you."

"He's not my son. And he doesn't owe me anything. He's…he's a good kid."

The paramedic looked at Pete askance.

"Okay, gramps, okay. Why don't you just let me put this mask on you?"

Pete said nothing, too weak to talk. All he had left was trust.

ABOUT THE AUTHOR

A lifelong historian and World War II buff, Christopher Mars is a high school teacher and lives in Lone Tree, Colorado with his wife, Elizabeth, and their three children. Despite growing up in Cleveland, Ohio, Chris always felt "haunted by mountains", which explains why he moved to Colorado, ran the Pikes Peak Marathon, and summited 48 of Colorado's 54 fourteeners (mountains above 14,000 feet in elevation).

CPSIA information can be obtained
at www.ICGtesting.com
Printed in the USA
LVHW031238130121
676355LV00005B/446